THE JUNIOR NOVEL

THE JUNIOR NOVEL

Adapted by Judy Katschke

HarperKidsEntertainment
An Imprint of HarperCollinsPublishers

Chapter One

Bump! Bump! Bump!

Ranger Beth bounced the heavy cooler down the steps of the cabin and then flung it into the back of her jeep. But as Beth arranged her cargo, she had no idea that she was being watched . . .

A few feet away a dark shadow crept out of the garage, moving straight toward Beth. It was the shadow of a grizzly bear—the most feared and ferocious animal in North America!

The grizzly loomed large behind Beth. He bared his razor-sharp teeth. He raised his eight-inch claws over Beth's unsuspecting head. Then he opened his cavernous mouth and Beth whirled around.

"Roooooooarrrrrr!" she bellowed.

The grizzly bear blinked in shock, his fur blown

back by the power of Beth's roar. Beth laughed. "Gotcha!" she said. "Now get in. We're gonna be late."

As Beth climbed into the driver's seat of the jeep, the enormous grizzly pouted. Then he decided to play it cool.

"No denyin', the girl's got growl," Boog said. "But can she get down like this?" Just as he started to dance, there was a loud *HONK!*

Boog jumped sky-high. Then the most feared animal in North America made a mad dash to the back of the jeep.

Beth fired up the engine and they were off!

Boog loved riding in Beth's jeep. He clutched the roll bar as it rambled along rocky roads toward the town of Timberline. Nestled at the foot of the Sawtooth Mountains and surrounded by lofty pines, Timberline was a sleepy little village—until Boog showed up!

Boog grinned as he wiggled his big furry behind at passing motorists. When the passengers saw the grizzly, they smiled and waved back. That's because Boog was not in the business of scaring anyone. His business was show business, and the only roar he cared about was that of the adoring crowd!

Beth steered the jeep onto Timberline's Main Street. It was usually as quiet as the village itself, but today the street was jumping with hunters gearing up for the big day. The opening of hunting season!

Boog watched the hunters in their flannel shirts. They didn't scare him. Open season was for wild animals and he was far from wild. From the day Beth rescued Boog as an orphaned cub, he had enjoyed a cushy garage apartment, eight square meals a day with snacks, and a hit stage show. People didn't want Boog's hide—they wanted his autograph!

Beth pulled the jeep into the parking lot of the outdoor ampitheater. The Fish and Game office was just a few feet away.

"Hey, Gordy!" Beth called with a wave.

Gordy, the town sheriff, stood on the porch. His dark eyes twinkled as he waved back.

"Mornin', Beth!" Gordy called.

He turned around to hang a wooden sign in the window that read in big bold letters:

OPEN SEASON IN THREE DAYS!

"Welcome to Timberline's Wilderness Extravaganza!" Beth announced from the stage. "I'm Ranger Beth!"

Beth stood in front of the curtain of the open-air theater. The wooden stage was flanked by two towering totem poles, and it was packed with curious and excited tourists.

"Today we're going to meet with North America's largest omnivore," Beth explained.

Backstage, Boog listened for his cue. He brushed off his fur and waved his grizzly tail back and forth. "Here we go," Boog said to himself. "My time to shine!"

"Behold," Beth announced with a sweep of her arm. "The mighty grizzly!"

All riiight! Boog thought. *Show time!*

A spotlight hit the back curtain.

The audience saw the giant shadow and gasped. When the shadow let out the most ear-splitting roar, they sprang to their feet!

The terrified men, women, and children were

about to bolt when the curtains parted and the mighty grizzly pedaled out on a teeny-tiny unicycle!

Boog felt the love as everyone clapped and cheered. He danced! He made funny faces at the audience! By the time he took his final bows, the bear knew he was a hit!

"We rocked that house, didn't we, Boog?" Beth said excitedly as they left the theater. "They were eating out of our hands . . . well, my hands, your paws!"

Beth's eyes lit up. "Hey, good one!" she said. "That's going in the next show." Boog rolled his eyes. He loved Beth, but her jokes weren't exactly hilarious.

All of a sudden Beth stopped in her tracks. Boog followed her disgusted gaze. Parked next to her jeep was a truck. Strapped to its hood was a deer, and the poor thing was missing an antler!

Beth narrowed her eyes. The truck belonged to Shaw, the meanest hunter in Timberline.

Shaw was as suspicious as he was mean. If it were up to Shaw, every wild beast would be stuffed and hanging on the wall of his hunting cabin.

"Shaw!" Beth spat. "That guy really chaps my khakis! You wait here, Boog."

Boog tried not to look at the deer as he climbed into the jeep. Other animals didn't interest him, especially dead-looking ones. Instead, Boog watched Beth as she marched toward the Fish and Game office. While waiting, he made himself comfortable in the back of the jeep.

If Boog was lucky, there would be some crackers inside. And if he was super-lucky, Beth would bring him back a little snack.

Boog's mouth watered like it always did when he thought about food. Meals were another great thing about living in the civilized world. With all those instant yummy treats, who needed to go fishing?

Beth slammed open the office door. She could see the back of Shaw's mullet as he stood in front of the sheriff's desk.

"Cuff him, Gordy!" Beth demanded.

Shaw turned around slowly. He smiled when he saw Beth.

"Oh," he sneered. "The Girl Scouts are here."

"He's at it again, Gordy," Beth said, pointing out the window.

Gordy stopped giving out hunting licenses long enough to glance out the window. When he saw Shaw's truck, he shook his head.

"Hunting season doesn't start for three days, Shaw," Gordy said. "What are you doing with that deer on the hood?"

Shaw's mouth dropped open as he faked surprise. "What?" he cried. "It isn't my fault. That thing ran right in front of my truck!"

"Where?" Gordy cried. "On the highway?"

Shaw smiled as he remembered the scene. It was the dark of night and he was driving along a mountain road. Suddenly, in the headlights he spotted the scrawniest mule deer in the world grazing off to the side. His truck lurched off the road and—*BAM*—right into the stunned deer!

"Sorta," Shaw lied.

Beth rolled her eyes. If it were up to her, Shaw's head would be the one hanging over a mantel in the hunting lodge!

Shaw wasn't crazy about Beth, either. If it were up to him, her pet grizzly Boog wouldn't be riding a

11

unicycle. He would be riding on the hood of his truck. Just like that scrawny buck he'd captured!

While Beth and Shaw locked horns, Boog waited outside in the jeep. *Where is that girl?* he muttered to himself.

Boog reached over and honked the horn. When Beth didn't come out, he leaned back and yawned. He was about to snooze when he heard a noise. Almost like a groan.

"What was that?" Boog gasped.

All he could see was the one-horned deer roped to the hood of the truck. Boog leaned over and took a whiff.

"Phew!" Boog said. "That thing is nasty!"

He picked up a twig and poked at the carcass. It looked dead. It acted dead. It even smelled dead. Until . . .

Blink!

One of its eyes popped open!

"Aaaaaahh!" Boog screamed.

"Aaaaaahh!" the deer screamed, too.

Boog freaked! The deer was *alive*!

Chapter Two

"What's going on?" the deer asked. He opened both eyes and stared at Boog.

"Where am I?"

The deer's name was Elliot. He had a big black nose, huge horrified eyes, and ears that jutted out like the wings on a plane on either side of his lone antler.

"I saw a bright light," Elliot said as he stared into the distance. "Then I saw two bright lights!" He looked right at Boog. "And . . . am I dead?"

"Not yet," Boog said. "But, seeing as that's Shaw's truck, it won't be long!"

"Shaw? What's a Shaw?" Elliot asked.

"Only the meanest hunter in town," Boog explained.

Elliot struggled against the ropes. "A hunter!" he cried. "Did he get you, too?"

Boog laughed. As if anyone would want to shoot him. Not only was this deer scrawny and smelly, he was totally clueless!

"You don't see me tied up, do you?" Boog asked coolly. "This is my ride," he said, leaning back into the jeep.

"Your . . . ride?" Elliot asked.

Boog rolled his big brown eyes. *What part of I'm-not-your-average-bear did this dude not get?*

"Yeah!" Boog said. "And this is my town. These are my people. This is where I reside." He laughed. "Nobody is hunting this bear!"

Elliot's eyes lit up. If this bear was so important, maybe he could pull a few strings. Or ropes!

"Can you untie me?" Elliot asked. "Please? No one is looking. Go ahead!"

"Sorry," Boog said, shaking his head. "Ain't gonna be able to do it."

Elliot began to sob. Without Boog's help, his days were numbered. "What am I going to do?" he blubbered. "I don't want to be mounted on a wall!"

"Oh, calm down! That's not going to happen," Boog said. He nodded at Elliot's single antler. "Not with that pathetic rack!"

"You mean my antlers?" Elliot asked. His eyes crossed as he gazed up at his head. "What about them?"

Boog swiveled the rearview mirror so Elliot could take a look. The deer stared at his reflection. Then he shrieked.

"Aaaaaaauuuuuughhh!!! I'm a Uni-horn!" Elliot yelled. "Don't look at me! I'm hideous! I'm a monster! A one-horned monster!" Elliot realized that he had lost one of his antlers when Shaw's truck hit him.

Plonk! Still sobbing, Elliot dropped his head on the hood of the car. Boog groaned under his breath. Of all the cars to park his truck next to—Shaw had to pick his!

Meanwhile, inside the Fish and Game office, the battle between Beth and Shaw raged on. . . .

"Tree hugger!" Shaw shouted.

"Knuckle dragger!" Beth shouted back.

"Veggie burger!" Shaw yelled.

"All right, you two," Gordy cut in. "That's enough!"

Shaw glared at Beth. "Listen, Girl Scout," he growled, "they're all dumb animals. I'm just respecting the laws of nature." Beth scowled and folded her arms. He continued, "Man on top, animals on the bottom.

"But your bear's special," Shaw went on with a smile. "He belongs somewhere in the middle—between two slices of rye smothered in gravy!"

Beth was so mad she wanted to spit. How dare Shaw compare her precious Boog to a sandwich!

"You're a sick puppy, Shaw," Beth snapped. "A sick, sick, twisted puppy!"

Beth turned on the heel of her ranger boot. She stormed out of the office, making sure to slam the door behind her.

"Put me down for a box of cookies, will ya, Girl Scout?" Shaw cackled after her.

Beth stomped all the way back to the jeep. "Six-toed gun monkey!" she muttered as she climbed into the front seat. "Come on, Boog. Let's get out of here!"

Fine with me, Boog thought. *Anything to be rescued from that crazy deer!*

But Elliot wasn't about to give up. He stretched out his neck and began to whisper.

"Come on! I'm begging you. Please! Just untie me. Pretty please! Pleeeeeease?"

Boog gritted his sharp teeth. By now, he would do anything to get Elliot to shut up. So he reached out his claw and slashed Elliot's ropes with a single swipe.

"Go on," Boog said, faking a smile. "Scamper on back to the woods, little buddy!"

It couldn't hurt to be nice. Boog figured he'd never see the deer again anyway.

Elliot leaped off the hood of the truck. He was free! Free! Free!

"One-horned freak," Boog mumbled as the jeep rolled off.

Elliot didn't hear the "freak" part. All he heard was the word "buddy."

"He called me 'buddy'!" Elliot cried with joy. "He called me 'buddy'!"

Through the window, Shaw had seen Boog untie Elliot.

The door of the Fish and Game office

slammed open and Shaw raced outside. He saw Beth and the bear speed away as his deer wiggled out of the ropes.

"My buck!" Shaw shouted.

Elliot took one look at Shaw and screamed! He knocked out a headlight with his hoof as he scampered away.

"My truck!" Shaw yelled. "Why you little—"

Just as Shaw was about to go after Elliot, a hand reached out to stop him.

"You know the rules, Shaw," Gordy said. "It's not hunting season yet."

Shaw groaned. His roadkill had hit the road!

"But that bear!" Shaw cried. "That bear untied him. Didn't you see?"

The other hunters on the porch chuckled.

"All I see is a busted headlight," Gordy said as he wrote up a ticket. "Shaw, you've been living in the woods too long."

Shaw crumpled up the ticket on the way to his truck. His eyes narrowed as he lifted the slashed rope.

"They can't tell me what I seen," Shaw muttered. "Because only I know what I seen."

It just served to confirm his theory that every animal was plotting to take over the human world. Seeing the bear free the deer was prime evidence! To Shaw, the only good animal was a dead animal. And he was going to make sure that Elliot—and Boog—fit that description fast!

That night, hunters were the last thing on Boog's mind. He was snug inside his garage apartment watching his favorite show, *Wheel of Fortune*.

"Big money going!" Boog shouted. "Come on! Come on!"

Beth walked in and snapped off the TV. "Okay, buddy," she said. "Time for bed."

Boog grumbled as he snapped the TV back on. Beth snapped it right off.

"Come on, Boog," Beth said. "Mr. Dinkelman is waiting."

Boog smiled. Mr. Dinkelman, or just Dinkelman, was a bear, too—a teddy bear. Boog had gotten him when he was a young cub, and he always felt nice and cozy with Dinkelman tucked under his arm.

Boog padded over to his bed. It was a doggy

bed and much too small for a grizzly. But to Boog, it was the place where sweet dreams were made.

As Boog snuggled with Dinkelman, Beth tucked him in. "Good night, big guy," she said softly.

Beth turned to leave. That's when she heard Boog whimper, as he did every night.

"Did I forget something?" Beth asked. She pulled a fishy cracker from her pocket and tossed it to Boog. He popped it into his mouth and swallowed it in a single gulp. Then he whimpered and growled for more.

"No more treats for you," Beth said firmly.

Yeah, right, Boog thought. He knew how to push Beth's buttons. All it took was a little face time . . .

Beth chuckled. Boog was rolling his big eyes and wiggling his fuzzy brow. "No, no, no!" She laughed. "Not the Face! It's not going to work this time. I'm serious, Boog. It's cute but—"

Boog tilted his head like a lovesick puppy. Beth was always a sucker for the Face!

"Oh, all right!" Beth laughed as she tossed Boog another cracker. After scarfing it down, Boog was finally ready for bed. Well, almost ready.

Beth pulled the string on Dinkelman's back. A tune jingled and she began to sing.

Boog listened to his favorite lullaby. It always made him feel as warm and fuzzy on the inside as he was on the outside. He closed his eyes as Beth's soothing voice lulled him to sleep.

"Good night, Boog," Beth whispered. She closed the door, leaving Boog alone in the garage. But he was not alone for long. . . .

Bonk! Bonk! Bonk!

Boog sat straight up in bed. What was that?

Bonk! Bonk! Bonk!

Boog turned his head. A white rabbit hit the window with a splat. Its face squished against the glass as it slid down slowly.

"Who's there?" Boog demanded.

More rabbits made splats against the window.

Boog's fur stood on end. He climbed out of bed and made his way toward the window.

"I-I'm warning you!" Boog called in a shaky voice. "I got ten claws and I'm not afraid to use them!"

The window flew open. A deer head with one

antler popped through. "Hey, buddy! It's me! Elliot!"

Boog jumped back. Was it really that crazy deer from the hood of Shaw's truck? Or was it his worst nightmare?

Chapter Three

"Hey, buddy, what are you doing here?" Boog demanded.

Elliot climbed through the window into the garage. "You helped me!" he explained. "So I'm returning the favor. I'm busting you out of here!"

"Busting me out?" Boog cried. *Where does this nutty dude think I am? In jail?*

Elliot ran behind Boog and pushed him toward the window. "Let's do it before the warden makes her rounds," he said. "Come on!"

"Warden? Whoa, whoa," Boog said. "You've got it all twisted, cornflake. This isn't the slammer. This is my home."

Elliot stopped pushing Boog. He looked around the junk-filled garage and said, "Sweet!"

"Now haul your butt back out that window!" Boog demanded. "Go ahead!"

Elliot wasn't going anywhere. Not until he checked out Boog's pad.

"Ooh!" Elliot said, scampering around the garage. "What's this?"

Boog watched as Elliot jumped up and down on his bed. "Hey!" he shouted. "Get off of that!"

"So soft!" Elliot swooned as he bounced. He stopped midair when his eye fell on something else. "What's that?"

Elliot raced into Boog's bathroom. He laughed as he unrolled reams and reams of toilet paper!

"Whoa! Whoa!" Boog shouted. "What are you doing in there?"

"Hey, you know," Elliot said as he ran out of the bathroom, "this place is big enough for two!"

"Two?" Boog cried.

Elliot began yanking stuff out of a big cardboard box. He pressed a clothes hanger against his head where his antler used to be.

"Does this look natural?" Elliot asked.

"Give me that!" Boog said, grabbing the hanger. He was about to toss it back into the box when—

"Ooh!" Elliot's voice said. "Who's this little guy?"

Boog looked up and gulped. Elliot was holding up his precious Dinkelman!

"Um . . . it's Dinkelman," Boog muttered.

Elliot stared at the plush bear. "Dinkelman?" he asked. "Is Dinkelman . . . your doll?"

Boog felt himself blush under his fur. Dinkelman wasn't a doll, he was a teddy bear. But that didn't sound too cool, either.

"Ah, I don't care about that old thing," Boog said.

"Okay," Elliot said. He tossed Dinkelman over his shoulder and Boog lunged to catch the teddy bear.

While Boog tucked Dinkelman into his bed, Elliot checked out the rest of the garage. Boog had a water bowl, a kibble bowl, and a doggy bed. That's when it finally clicked.

"Oh, I get it," Elliot said. "You're like some kind of pet!"

Pet? The word made Boog steam. Pets were little yappy things on leashes! Pets wore licenses around their necks! Pets had cutesy little names like Fluffy and Muffin!

"I am nobody's pet!" Boog declared.

Elliot dangled the kibble bowl from his hoof. Boog's name was written on it.

"Yeah, riiiiight!" Elliot said.

Boog snatched back the bowl. "Let's get one thing straight," he snapped. "I do what I want when I want. I come and go as I please!"

"Okay," Elliot said. He swung the garage door wide open. "Then let's go."

Go? Boog looked past the garage door. Outside was dark and cold. Inside was nice and warm.

"Why would I want to go outside when I have everything I need in here?" Boog asked nervously.

Just then, Boog's big, black nose began to twitch. It sniffed and dragged Boog across the garage to the door where Elliot stood holding a chocolate bar.

"What's that?" Boog gulped. He didn't usually eat candy; Beth always gave him healthy treats.

Elliot pulled off the shiny foil wrapper and took a bite. "I call them Woo-Hoos," he said between chews. "Like, woo-hooooo! You want one?"

Boog's nose twitched faster and faster, like some candy-detecting radar!

"I know where there's a bunch of them," Elliot said slowly. He held the bar close to Boog's nose. "But you have to go outside to get them."

Boog frowned. This was just a sneaky trick to get him to leave the garage . . . and it was working!

"Stop it!" Boog cried. He slapped his twitching nose with his paws. "Stop it, stupid nose!"

"Inside . . . outside. Inside . . . outside," Elliot said as he waved the candy bar in and out of the door. "What will it be?"

Boog couldn't stand it. He snatched the candy bar and shoved it into his mouth. A few seconds later he felt like he was floating on a heavenly chocolate cloud. He had never tasted anything so good!

"Woo-hoo!" Boog shouted through a mouth full of chocolate. "Woo-hooooooooo!"

Elliot smiled. Boog had his first taste of the incredibly yummy Woo-Hoo bar. Next stop: his first taste of *freedom*!

Chapter Four

"Over there!" Elliot whispered. "I got the Woo-Hoo bar from one of those container doohickies."

It was the middle of the night. Boog and Elliot were on Main Street. They were in a dark alley, peering over a car at a Dumpster.

"What?" Boog hissed. "You got it out of the garbage? I had it in my mouth and everything!"

Suddenly Boog's nose twitched wildly. It picked Boog up and dragged him toward the PuniMart grocery store as if it had a mind of its own!

"Dude!" Elliot said as he followed. "You're freaking me out with that nose thing!"

Boog's runaway nose landed flat against the store window. When Boog looked inside, he saw shelves filled with candy bars.

"Whoa!" Boog cried. "It's a whole Woo-Hoo village!"

"Sweet!" Elliot said.

Boog had to get inside. He raced to the door and pulled the handle. "It's locked," he said. "Maybe we should come back tomorrow."

But Elliot had a plan. He grabbed a shopping cart and charged toward the PuniMart full speed ahead. Then he crashed the cart right through the front door!

Boog couldn't believe it. First Elliot broke into his garage—and now a grocery store. Was there any place this deer *wouldn't* go?

Boog's nose was still twitching, but he called inside: "Elliot! Look what you did! You're going to get us into trouble. . . ." He tried to resist, but it was no use. His nose was under the spell of the cookies, crackers, and the candy section.

Shoving Elliot out of the way, Boog dashed straight for the candy. He sang to himself as he scooped dozens of chocolate bars into his arms. . . .

"The Woo-Hoo bar's my laaa-dy!" Boog opened

his mouth and let the bars tumble in. He chomped, swallowed, and let out a huge *hiccup*!

Meanwhile Elliot was busy at the frozen drink machine, pulling levers and pushing buttons. Bright green goo gushed out of the machine and onto the floor.

"What is this thing?" Elliot wondered.

"Let me try!" Boog said. He shoved Elliot out of the way and filled his open mouth with the green slush. It was cold and, oh, so sweet!

If this is what it's like to be free, Boog thought, *sign me up!*

Boog and Elliot were on a roll. Next the two gulped gas from a helium balloon tank. The stuff made their voices sound high and squeaky.

"Hello, idiot!" Boog squeaked.

"It's Elliot!" Elliot squeaked back. They both laughed.

While Elliot got busy stylin' at the sunglass rack, Boog discovered the wonders of bubblegum. He chewed a wad and blew a humongous bubble. When it burst, it covered him with a sticky pink web!

But the fun had just begun. It was time to *par-tay!*

The animals danced the night away on top of the counter. They squirted each other with cheese in a can. They gulped down sugar from hundreds of sugar packets. They tore open cereal boxes and potato chip bags, covering the floor until they could lie down and make snow angels in the junk food.

It was definitely a case of animals gone wild. That is, until Elliot saw flashing red lights outside the window.

"Boog! Boog!" Elliot said. "Party's over. Let's get out of here!"

"Oh, yeah! All riiiiight!" Boog sang as he galloped around the store riding a golf club like a horse. Nothing could stop this party animal now, not even the blaring of Gordy's police siren.

"I'm outta here!" Elliot said as he bolted out the back door.

Boog kept right on partying—until he heard the word, "Freeze!"

A spotlight hit Boog and he grinned. Then he spun around and announced in a sugar–induced haze: "Behold! The mighty grizzly . . . good night."

Boog collapsed in a heap of junk food. The next thing he knew, he was sitting in the back of Gordy's jeep and gulping down a box of animal crackers.

"Hey! The giraffe tastes just like the elephant!" Boog complained. "That's messed up!"

Gordy didn't say a word as he pulled into Beth's driveway. Boog gulped when he saw Beth. She was standing in front of the garage with a scowl on her face.

"Uh, oh," Boog said. "Back up! Before she sees me!"

Too late. Beth marched to the back of the jeep and pulled the door open. Boog spilled out on the driveway.

"Say—whaaaaa?" Boog slurred.

Beth looked down at the big bear, who was lying on the pavement making growling noises.

"You are in big trouble, mister!" Beth scolded. She picked empty sugar packets off of his fur. "Boog! You know what sugar does to you," she said angrily. "Straight to bed. Now!"

Boog stumbled to his feet. Muttering under his breath, he lumbered to the garage.

"I am so sorry, Gordy," Beth said. "It won't happen again."

"What if Boog had hurt someone?" Gordy asked.

Hurt? Beth shook her head. Boog wasn't a ferocious grizzly bear. He was a unicycle-riding marshmallow puff!

"Gordy, please," Beth said. "We're talking about Boog here. He's been with me since I rescued him when he was just an orphaned cub."

"I know, Beth," Gordy said gently. "But when you found him as a cub, we agreed you would one day put him back where he belongs. It's time now."

Beth's eyes flew wide open. She knew she'd hear those words sooner or later. She had just hoped it would be later. Or never!

"You mean . . . out in the wild?" Beth gasped. She shook her head. "No, no, no. Boog isn't ready to go back yet!"

Boog could be heard in the garage as he

growled to Dinkelman, "What are you looking at?"

Beth and Gordy turned toward the garage. Boog was hurling junk out of the door—not a very civilized thing for a civilized bear to do!

"I tried to teach him the basics, Gordy," Beth said. "I took him fishing, but he didn't want to get wet."

"Beth, you're not his mother," Gordy said.

"I'm not mothering him," Beth insisted. She turned to the garage and saw Boog looking out the window. He tried to flash her the Face—but all he could do was barf.

"Just one more summer, Gordy!" Beth pleaded. "That's all I'm asking."

Gordy opened his mouth to speak.

"Great!" Beth cut in. "See? I can be reasonable. Thanks, Gordy!"

Beth began walking back to the house.

"You know, Beth," Gordy called after her, "the longer you wait, the harder it's going to be for Boog to adapt."

"Oh, I'm sure he will be fine," Beth said.

"And the longer you wait," Gordy went on, "the harder it's going to be for you to let him go."

Beth stopped walking. She watched in silence

as Gordy's jeep drove away. Deep inside she knew Gordy was right. But how could she ever give up her precious little cub?

Beth walked into the garage and sat next to Boog. He sure wasn't a cub anymore—even if he did act like a big baby once in a while.

"Oh, Boog." Beth sighed. "What am I going to do with you?"

Chapter Five

Shaw drove his truck down Main Street. As he passed the PuniMart he saw a group of townsfolk huddled together. The store was a disaster and yellow police tape was wound around the doors.

"Did you hear?" one was saying. "Boog got loose last night and totally trashed the place."

Shaw's eyebrows arched. *Boog?*

"Hmm," Shaw said. "There's something going on here."

At that same time, Elliot was strutting out of an alley. He had spent the rest of the night in a Dumpster and was now drinking from a discarded coffee cup. He had never sipped from a no-foam-skinny latté before. But he was definitely hooked!

"Mmm," Elliot said. He was about to take

another sip when his eyes met Shaw's.

"Aaaaaahh!" Elliot screamed.

Shaw stared at the coffee-toting deer who was standing on two legs. The deer had one antler, which meant it was his buck that had gotten away!

"You!" Shaw growled. "It walks like a man!" Seeing a deer walk like a man, Shaw was now positive that the animals were plotting together. He had to do something!

Elliot took one last slurp of his latté, then began to run. Shaw jammed his foot on the gas pedal and steered his truck straight toward Elliot!

"Hold still," Shaw shouted, "you two-legged latté drinker!"

Elliot hightailed it past the Fish and Game office. Gordy stirred in his porch rocking chair as Shaw's truck barreled after the deer.

"Not again," Gordy groaned.

Back at the ampitheater, the show had to go on. . . .

"Boog will have you eating out of his paw," Beth

joked to the audience. "Get it? Because he's . . . a bear?"

The audience was silent. Beth knew she was bombing big-time. But what did she expect? They weren't there to see Beth the forest ranger. They were there to see Boog, the mighty grizzly!

"Oh, man," Boog moaned backstage.

He rubbed his throbbing head. It was the last time he would party with Elliot. If he was lucky, last night would be the last time he would ever *see* Elliot!

"Relax," Boog told himself. "You can do this."

He was about to make his entrance when Elliot tore through the backstage door. Panting, the deer slammed the stage door shut and clicked the lock.

"Aaaaaahh!" Boog cried. "What are you doing here?"

"You've got to help! I've got to hide!" Elliot yelled.

Boog stared at Elliot. Why would he want to help Elliot with anything? Especially after the mess he had gotten Boog into last night.

"Get out of here!" Boog ordered.

Elliot jumped up on Boog's back. "He's right behind me!" he hissed.

"Who is?" Boog asked.

A loud banging noise made them jump. Someone was trying to break down the door.

Outside, Shaw peeked in the window. When he saw Boog and Elliot together, he scowled.

"I knew it," Shaw said. "That bear has corrupted my buck!"

Shaw banged on the door again.

"Aaaaaahh!" Elliot screamed. "You've got to hide me!"

The banging suddenly stopped. Boog waited a few seconds. Then he turned to Elliot, pointed to the door, and said, "He's gone. Now get out!"

"Good idea!" Elliot said.

But instead of running out the door, Elliot dashed through the curtains and onto the stage— just as the spotlight flashed on.

"Where are you going?" Boog shouted. His frantic shadow was outlined against the curtain as Beth announced, "Behold! The mighty grizzly!"

Confused whispers filled the theater.

"Huh?" Beth turned and saw a scrawny mule deer standing next to her. Where did he come from?

"Um . . . roar?" Elliot gulped.

The audience laughed at the funny-looking animal with one antler.

"Isn't he sweet?" a woman cooed.

"What is he?" a man asked. "Some kind of donkey?"

Elliot flashed a few goofy faces at the crowd for more laughs. But Elliot wasn't laughing when Boog reached out and yanked him behind the curtain.

"You got me in enough trouble!" Boog growled. He held Elliot up against the wall.

"Hey, you saved my life!" Elliot said. "That means you're responsible for me!"

"Stop messing up my life!" Boog ordered.

"You needed to get out of that prison," Elliot reminded. "You should thank me!"

"Thank you?!" Boog cried.

Elliot smiled and said, "You're welcome, buddy."

Boog gritted his teeth so hard they almost

cracked. "Stop calling me that!" he said. "Now get out!"

"But I need to hide!" Elliot whined. Boog lunged for Elliot and chased him as the deer ran around.

Their two shadows appeared clearly on the curtain for everyone to see. The audience gasped.

"Boog?" Beth said.

Boog let out a bloodcurdling roar as Elliot jumped into an old cabinet.

"Oh, no, you don't!" Boog said. "You're leaving now!"

Boog yanked Elliot out of the cabinet. The deer was hiding in an old coat wrapped around his scrawny body.

"Out of the coat!" Boog shouted.

"No!" Elliot said.

Boog struggled to tear the coat off Elliot. From the other side of the curtain, watching their shadows, it looked like Boog was ripping off the poor animal's fur! The audience gasped again.

"He's eating the donkey!" a voice shouted.

"He's going to eat us all!" another one cried.

Elliot dove into a pile of rope. "You know,

41

Shaw's still out there!" he said.

Boog pulled at the rope, trying to get at Elliot. To the audience it looked like Boog was yanking out the poor animal's guts!

"Boog, what are you doing?" Beth shouted. "Put that animal down this instant!"

But Boog was too busy chasing Elliot to hear Beth.

"Hold still!" Boog shouted. "You're ruining my show!"

"I'm staying!" Elliot insisted.

Beth continued to watch from the stage. "Sit, Boog!" she ordered. "You're getting a time out for this. I'm really getting angry!"

Elliot scampered up a wall onto a shelf. A large paint can tipped over, splattering the outside of the curtain with bright red paint.

"Blood!" a woman shouted.

The audience jumped to their feet. They stampeded toward the exit.

"No, wait!" Beth called out.

The backstage drama continued to build.

"I'm going to kill you!" Boog shouted.

The fleeing crowd turned just in time to see

the shadow of Boog rising on his hind legs. The mighty grizzly was poised to attack!

"Stay calm! Stay calm!" Beth called to the audience. "He's harmless. Really!"

One person shoved his way through the crowd toward the stage. It was Shaw!

"Out of my way! Move!" Shaw shouted. "Show's over, you freaks of nature!"

Shaw saw Boog grab Elliot by the throat. He aimed his hunting rifle at Boog. Then he peered through the gun scope. He was about to get a clear shot when . . .

"Shaw, drop that gun!" Gordy ordered.

Shaw didn't hear the sheriff. All he could hear was the sound of Boog growling at Elliot and people screaming.

"Easy now," Shaw told himself. "Just line them up."

Shaw steadied the barrel. He lifted his finger to pull back the trigger.

Bang!

Chapter Six

"Oooh," Boog cried, suddenly woozy and sleepy. "Buttermilk biscuit!"

He fell to the floor, a bright red dart sticking out of his neck.

Gordy had pushed Shaw's gun down, so Shaw hadn't been the one to shoot. Gordy and Shaw whipped around to see Beth holding a tranquilizing dart gun. *She* had fired the shot that took Boog down.

Boog tumbled on top of Elliot. The deer was struggling out from under Boog when—

Thunk!

A dart hit Elliot in the butt. He waved his front legs in the air as four more darts hit him. *Thunk! Thunk! Thunk! Thunk!*

"Ooh! Ooh!" Elliot cried as he fell to the floor.

Both animals were down for the count. But Gordy and Shaw couldn't take their eyes off Beth as she clutched her gun. She had never shot anyone or anything before, not even with a tranquilizer!

Beth couldn't believe it either!

"Shaw, you're under arrest," Gordy said. But when he turned his head, Shaw was already gone.

Gordy walked over to Beth. The ranger's hands were trembling as she stared at the shadows of Boog and Elliot and said, "I didn't know what else to do."

"It's time, Beth," Gordy said.

"But . . . what about hunting season?" Beth asked.

"Take him above the falls," Gordy advised. "He'll be safe there."

Beth's shoulders drooped. She wished she could keep Boog forever, but in her aching heart she knew it was time for him to go home.

At sunset Beth piloted a Ranger Service helicopter deep into the Sawtooth Mountains. Hanging from the chopper was a net. Sleeping peacefully inside the net was Boog.

Beth steered the helicopter above a beautiful mountain meadow and waterfall. The grass was as lush as velvet and the water shimmered like crystal. Brilliantly colored wildflowers dotted the landscape for miles.

I hope Boog likes it here, Beth thought with a heavy heart.

After lowering the net to the ground, Beth landed the helicopter and climbed out. She uncovered Boog's sleeping face and whispered, "You're going to be fine."

Beth's eyes watered as she nestled Dinkelman next to Boog. "I'm going to miss you, big guy," she said softly.

After hugging Boog for a long time, Beth ran to the chopper. For Beth, it was the end of a difficult day. For Boog, it was the beginning of a whole new life.

When morning arrived, Boog opened one eye and yawned. The first thing he saw was Dinkelman. The next thing he saw was a brilliant purple wildflower.

"Pretty," Boog grunted.

He heard his stomach growl. Beth was probably

preparing his breakfast now. Boog sniffed at the fragrant bloom.

Wait a minute, Boog thought. *Since when do flowers grow in the garage?*

Both eyes popped wide open as he snapped awake. His heart thumped faster and faster as he looked around. He wasn't in the garage at all. He was in the middle of the wilderness—the middle of nowhere!

"Aaaaahh!" Boog screamed. "Where's home? It's gone! Somebody stole home!"

Yawning, Elliot's head rose out of the bag right next to Boog. "Hey, can you keep it down?" he said. "I'm trying to sleep in here."

"You!" Boog shouted. He grabbed Elliot's antler and ripped him out of the bag.

Snapping awake, Elliot yelled, "I didn't do it!"

Boog hauled Elliot to the edge of a cliff. He dangled him over by his antler and said, "Take a good look, Elliot! What do you see, Elliot? Something's missing, Elliot! What is it, Elliot? *What is it?*"

Elliot looked down and gulped.

"Wait, don't tell me," he said, thinking hard.

"Timberline is missing!" Boog shouted.

"Um . . . I was just going to say that," Elliot squeaked.

"My garage is missing!" Boog screamed. "My breakfast, lunch, and dinner are missing! My life is missing, and it's all your fault!"

Boog dropped Elliot off the cliff. The deer screamed until Boog caught him with his other claw.

"You're funny," Elliot gasped. "I thought maybe you might drop me, but then again I—"

Boog tossed Elliot over his shoulder.

"This has to be a mistake!" Boog told himself. "Think, Boog. She's mad at you, but you can fix it. Just give her the Face. That's it! The Face never fails!"

Boog dumped Elliot on the ground. He landed headfirst, his one antler stuck in the mud.

"I've got to get back before Beth forgets the Face," Boog said. "That'll make everything okay!"

"Boog, you don't know where you're going," Elliot shouted after him. "You can't just go wandering around out here! Boog!"

"I'm going home," Boog muttered back.

Elliot tried to pop out of the ground, but it was no use. "Wait, Boog!" he shouted. "I know where Timberline is. I can bring you back. Wait!"

Boog kept on walking. He unzipped Dinkelman's belly and pulled out two bands. Then he strapped the teddy bear onto his back as a backpack.

Shoving the brush aside, Boog left the clearing. Timberline couldn't be that far. It had to be around somewhere!

But after trekking for what seemed like miles, Boog finally realized what was wrong. He was walking around in circles!

"Okay," Boog said, exhausted. "I have to get the lay of the land. Maybe if I get up high enough, I'll be able to see Timberline."

Boog glanced all the way up a tall tree.

"Hmm," Boog said. "I can climb this."

He whipped out his sharp claws and reached for the tree trunk. No problem. Bears were supposed to climb trees. How else would they get all that honey? Honey did grow on trees . . . didn't it? Whatever.

But just as Boog was about to dig in—

"Oi! Lost your way to Sunday School, pal?" a

strange voice shouted out from the treetop.

"Huh?" Boog asked. He looked all the way up and spotted a squirrel, hopping out on a branch. It had a bushy tail and even bushier eyebrows!

The squirrel puffed out his chest. "This is McSquizzy's turf," he declared in a thick Scottish accent. "And nobody messes with McSquizzy, because that's me!"

"What?" Boog asked. He moved toward the tree but didn't get far.

"Touch one needle on this tree and I'll give you such a doin'!" McSquizzy warned.

Boog glared up at the squirrel. He wasn't the boss of him!

"Oh, yeah?" Boog shouted. "You and what army?"

McSquizzy let out a shrill whistle. In a flash, an army of squirrels appeared on the branches.

"Mess not with the Furry Tail Clan," McSquizzy said. "Defenders of the Good, Crusaders of the Righteous, Guardians of the Pine!"

Boog rolled his eyes. This guy was as nuts as the stuff he stashed away! "Aw, keep your tree," he said. "I'll just find another one."

As Boog turned to leave, McSquizzy spotted the teddy bear strapped to Boog's back. He jumped up and down, chattering with laughter.

"Look!" McSquizzy shouted. "He's got a wee freakish twin growing out of his back!"

The other squirrels yukked it up, too.

Laugh all you want, Boog thought. *There are other trees in this thing they call a forest.*

He walked toward another tree.

Bonk! Boog saw stars as an acorn whopped him in the head.

"Try it again and I'll be kicking your furry brown bahookie!" McSquizzy warned.

"This is a *different* tree!" Boog cried, rubbing his aching head.

"They're all my trees!" McSquizzy said. "I suggest you turn around and go back where you came from."

"That's what I'm trying to do," Boog said. "Just point the way to town and I'll be out of here!"

The squirrels chortled as they pointed in different directions.

"That's it," Boog said. "You asked for it!"

Boog grabbed the tree trunk.

"Ready, aim, fire!" McSquizzy shouted.

Nearby, Elliot was still trying to pull his head out of the mud when he heard a weird noise. It sounded like a hailstorm.

What is that? Elliot wondered.

He got his answer when Boog burst through the brush covered with acorns!

"Hey, Boog, look. No hands!" Elliot joked. He raised his hooves in the air. Next he pointed to his butt. "I think I'm getting a sunburn. Or should I say, moon burn!"

Boog wasn't in the mood for jokes. He shook off the acorns and grabbed Elliot by the tail. He yanked the deer out of the mud and shook him until his eyes rattled inside his head.

"Look!" Boog demanded. "Just give me the directions! I have to get back!"

"So sad." Elliot sighed.

Boog hated the wild. And he hated Elliot. But most of all he hated that he wasn't in his nice cozy garage, eating breakfast and watching his favorite TV shows!

"*Elliot!*" Boog shouted at the top of his lungs. "*Where is Timberline?*"

Chapter Seven

Elliot tried to calm Boog down.

"Okay, okay," he said gently. "You had it pretty good in Timberline, right?"

Boog stopped shaking Elliot. A giant lump formed in his throat as he thought about the good life.

"You had all the food you could eat," Elliot reminded, "Woo-Hoo bars, and you had safety . . . right?"

"Yeah." Boog sighed.

"But still something was missing," Elliot said.

Boog stared at Elliot. Missing? How could anything be missing? He had everything a bear could ask for back home.

"There was?" Boog asked. "What?"

Elliot flashed a grin. "Me! I'll take you home, Boog, but when we get there, we're partners. Deal?"

Boog dropped Elliot on the ground with a *thunk*.

"What?" he cried. "No! That will never, ever happen!"

"Come on, come on," Elliot urged.

"Don't you have a herd to get back to?" Boog asked.

Elliot gulped when he thought of his herd. How could he tell Boog the truth—that he had been kicked out of the herd? That he was a loser? He couldn't do it.

"Oh, my herd will understand," Elliot lied. "These guys are my buddies. They want the best for me."

"Forget it!" Boog snapped.

"Oh, well." Elliot sighed again. "You better start moving then," he said, pretending he didn't really care. "Open season starts in a few days." Elliot stared into Boog's eyes. "Maybe one of those hunters can give you a ride back—on the hood of his truck!"

The thought of being roped to a hunter's truck made Boog's stomach flip. He wanted to go home, but not that way!

"Hunters," Boog mumbled. "Okay, okay."

"Do we have a deal, then?" Elliot asked excitedly. He spit on his hoof and held it out. "Let me hear you say it!"

"You're disgusting," Boog said.

"Can't hear you!" Elliot taunted.

Boog took a deep breath. The last thing he wanted to do was buddy-up with this one-antlered jerk. But he did want to get back to Timberline.

"I guess," Boog muttered. "We can be . . . partners."

"Partners?" Elliot repeated.

Boog grabbed Elliot's hoof and said, "Partners."

Elliot wanted to jump for joy. His life was about to change and it was going to be awesome! He immediately puffed up his chest and took charge.

"Okeydokey!" Elliot said. "This way. Move it or lose it!"

As the two trekked into the forest, Elliot babbled nonstop about his hopes and dreams.

"I was thinking we should have a secret

handshake and nicknames!" Elliot said. "Cool nicknames, like, I can call you Boogster and you can call me the Incredible Mister E. I made that up. Isn't that great?"

Boog was trying hard to grin and bear it.

It wasn't easy!

"This is going to be awesome," Elliot went on. "It'll be just you and me. Hey, who's the lady with the shorts?"

Boog didn't bother explaining Beth. He was too busy wondering what he just got himself into. Why hadn't he just left Elliot stuck in the ground?

The two animals went on their way searching for home. In the meantime, a determined hunter was searching for *them*!

"They've been out here all night," Shaw mumbled to himself as he drove his truck up the mountain road. "A bear and a deer, working together. What other animals are involved in this conspiracy?"

Shaw gazed out the windshield. A camper was rambling up ahead at a slow pace. Stepping on the gas, Shaw tried to overtake it.

A tiny bit of doubt crept in. "Maybe everybody's

right," Shaw muttered as he passed the camper. "Maybe old Shaw is crazy. Maybe—"

Shaw turned his head and gasped. Sitting behind the wheel of the camper was a little brown dachshund!

"Wha—?" Shaw cried.

"Woof!" the dog barked.

Shaw lost control of the pickup truck. It careened off the road and down the hillside. Shaw's heart pounded as the truck came to a stop in the trees. He hadn't noticed that the dog had been sitting on its owner's lap, but it didn't matter. To Shaw, it was all part of the plot.

"Animals driving campers!" Shaw said through gritted teeth. "Next they'll be driving humans right out of town!"

Shaw gripped the steering wheel so hard it almost cracked. He was the only one who could stop them. He *had* to find that bear and that deer.

Chapter Eight

"Okay," Elliot said. "Forest 101."

Boog wiggled his itchy nose. He didn't want to be schooled on the subject of nature. He just wanted to get home!

"Ahh-chooo!" Boog sneezed.

"These big wood things are called trees," Elliot said, pointing in the distance.

"Got it." Boog sniffed.

Elliot ran up the cliff like a billy goat.

"And these big rocks are called mountains," Elliot pointed out. "The little rocks are their babies."

Boog huffed and puffed as he struggled to climb after Elliot. The altitude made his arms wobble like jelly.

"No jelly arm," Boog wheezed. "Come on."

Suddenly Boog lost his grip. He felt himself sliding!

"Elliot!" Boog shouted. He grabbed onto a root and hung from the face of the cliff.

Elliot peered down. "Boogster!" he shouted. "How many times do I have to tell you? I'm not Elliot—I'm the Incredible Mister E!"

"Elliot, please!" Boog shouted. He felt the root beginning to rip.

"Look," Elliot rambled on, "if you're not going to use the code names, how am I going to know who I'm really talking to?"

The root tore off the cliff. Boog screamed as he tumbled down the mountainside. He landed on top of a tree and crashed down from branch to branch.

"Ooof!" Boog grunted. *"Ugh! Oof!"*

When Boog landed, he opened his eyes and looked down. The branch he hung from was only two feet off the ground.

Boog slowly lowered himself just as a baby porcupine waddled over and stopped to sniff a flower right under Boog.

"Aaaaahh!" Boog screamed, as he landed on the baby porcupine and its needle-sharp quills.

With the prickly porcupine stuck to his butt, Boog hopped up and down. Could things in the wild get any worse?

"Just rip it off, Elliot," Boog pleaded. He stuck his prickly butt way out. "Like a bandage!"

"Hold still," Elliot advised. "Just be calm. This might pinch a little." There was a pause. "You might want to cover your ears."

Boog looked over his shoulder and groaned. Elliot wasn't talking to him—he was talking to the porcupine!

"Just get it over with!" Boog yelled.

Elliot spit on his hooves. Then he grabbed the porcupine and ripped it off of Boog's throbbing behind.

"Aaaaahh!" Boog screamed.

Elliot set the porcupine gently on the ground. "Okay, little buddy," he said. "Scamper on back to the woods."

As the little porcupine watched Boog and Elliot walk away, his face broke into a big smile. "Buddee," the lonely porcupine repeated fondly.

* * *

At a nearby river, a team of beavers were hard at work building a sturdy dam. Standing on top of the log pile and shouting out orders was their boss, Reilly.

"Okay, ladies!" Reilly shouted through his buckteeth. "This dam won't build itself. Lift that birch, swing those pines over here."

The busy beavers used their long, flat tails to stack the logs.

"Yo! O'Toole!" Reilly bellowed.

"Yeah, boss?" the young beaver asked.

"I want you to cantilever that cedar on the bias down by the north end," Reilly said. "You got that?"

"Huh?" O'Toole said.

"Put a twig in the hole!" Reilly shouted.

"Oh," O'Toole said as he scampered off.

"Rookie," Reilly mumbled. Then he turned to his crew and shouted, "Take five for lunch!"

The beavers sat in a row on the edge of the dam. They took out their lunches.

"What do you have?" Reilly asked.

"Wood," O'Toole replied. "How about you? Whatta you got?"

"Wood," Reilly said, looking at O'Toole's lunch.

"Want to trade?"

Suddenly Reilly spotted something in the distance. It was a bear and a deer walking past the dam. He stared at the big brown grizzly and grinned. A beaver didn't see *that* every day!

"Hey, guys, check it out!" Reilly shouted. "The largest omnivore in North America, the mighty grizzly!"

"Wow!" the other beavers murmured.

Elliot heard the beavers and smiled. He pointed to Boog and said, "And he's a good dancer. We're going to be in a show!"

The beavers cracked up laughing.

"Oh, yeah?" Reilly guffawed. "What does he do? Ride a unicycle?"

"Well . . . " Elliot started to say, but Boog wasn't about to let the wild animals hear about his life in Timberline. He wanted to keep it to himself.

He grabbed Elliot by his antler and began dragging him away.

"Ow, ow!" Elliot said. "That's my good antler!"

Boog slammed Elliot down. He looked deep into the deer's eyes and said, "Listen. We are not *we*! It's just *me*! And we are not doing a show!"

"Diva," Elliot muttered.

"What did you just call me?" Boog demanded.

Elliot sighed. "I understand what's going on here," he said. "You're a little crabby because you're hungry. Hmm?"

Boog could hear his stomach growl. He hadn't had anything yummy to eat since that out-of-control night at the PuniMart.

"I'm starving!" Boog cried.

Elliot whipped out a pinecone. "Here," he said. "Try this."

Boog stared at the pinecone. What was he, some kind of chipmunk? "I can't eat that!" he said.

"Picky, picky, picky." Elliot sighed. "Well, what do bears eat?"

Boog gave it a thought. All he knew about other bears beside himself were the ones he saw on the Nature Channel. Wait, didn't the bears on that one show go fishing?

"Um . . . bears eat . . . fish!" Boog said. "That's it. Bears eat fish!"

In just minutes Boog was standing on the edge of a river. For the first time in his life he actually looked and felt like a wild grizzly bear!

"All right, fishies!" Boog shouted. "Give it up for Boog!"

Three salmon leaped out of the water.

"Hee-*yaaa!*" they shouted as their tails slapped Boog silly.

Boog collapsed in the water with a huge *splash!* So much for a fish dinner. And so much for feeling like a real grizzly!

As the travelers moved on, Boog gnawed on a dry, tasteless pinecone. He was drenched, exhausted, and pretty ticked off. He also had a new problem. . . .

"Um," Boog said. "Hey, Incredible Mister E?"

"Yes, Boogster?" Elliot asked.

"I've . . . got to go," Boog said in a low voice.

"Then go!" Elliot shrugged.

"You don't get it," Boog said. "I need a toilet."

"A toilet?" Elliot asked. "What's a toilet?"

"You know," Boog said. "A think tank. The johnny-on-the-spot. The oval office!"

Elliot shook his head and said, "There's nothing like that out here."

"Then what do I do?" Boog cried.

Elliot slapped Boog on the back. "Don't look

now," he said, "but I see a little bush with your name written all over it!"

"A bush?" Boog cried. He stared at the thorny little shrub the deer was pointing to. Was Elliot serious? He could do without his bed for awhile. He could even do without his kibble bowl. But he couldn't do without a toilet bowl!

Chapter Nine

"Go on, Boog. It's just like riding a bike," Elliot urged.

Boog didn't want to do it. But when a bear has to go—he has to go! So he swallowed his pride and lumbered over to the bush. After trying to get comfortable, he asked, "Now what?"

"Show us your 'grrr' face, nature boy!" Elliot cheered. "Grrr! Grrr!"

Boog was about to "grr" when a rabbit hopped over. Then another rabbit. And another. And another—until twenty-five fluffy white rabbits were standing around Boog.

"Hey, what are you doing here?" Boog demanded. "Go away! Shoo! Shoo! I'm working here!"

Elliot rushed over. He shooed the curious rabbits away. "Okay, okay, you've had your fun," he said. "Nothing to see here. Let a bear do his thing."

The rabbits hopped away. Elliot leaned on a tree and shook his head. "Do you believe those guys?" he asked.

Boog couldn't believe it. He always loved having an audience, but not this way!

Then he looked at Elliot, who was staring at him, too. "Finished?" asked Elliot. Boog turned away.

"Grrrr!" Boog began to grunt. He had no clue that McSquizzy and the Furry Tail Clan were eyeballing him from the top of a tree.

"I bet me nuts that big hairy choob can't do it," McSquizzy said.

"I'll take a piece of the action!" another squirrel said.

Boog heard the squirrels chortling. He glanced up and yelled, "What's wrong with you animals?!"

"Maybe you need some fiber, buddy," Elliot suggested.

Boog didn't need fiber. Just privacy. He was

about to "grr" again when a small creature emerged from the bush. To Boog it looked like a squirrel with a white stripe down its back.

"What are you doing sitting on my house?" she demanded to know.

"This is your house?" Boog asked. He looked down and saw that he wasn't sitting on a bush. It was a tree stump. "Oh, I didn't know."

Another bushy-tailed creature strolled by. "It would probably be an improvement, Maria!" she said.

"What did you just say to me, Rosie?" Maria demanded. "You better watch your mouth or you're going to get yourself in a lot of trouble, girlfriend!"

Boog rolled his eyes.

Elliot called out from behind him, "What's the deal, Boogster?"

"I dunno, some kind of chick fight," Boog called back. Then he added, "What do I do?"

"You have to mark your territory!" Elliot called back. "Go ahead and show them who's boss!"

Boog looked down at the animals. "Okay, ladies," he said. "I'm laying down the law."

Maria and Rosie stopped fighting. They turned their backs to Boog and lifted their tails.

Elliot added, "Unless, of course, they're skunks."

Sssss! Boog gagged as a spray of stink hit him squarely in the face.

"*Now* you tell me, Elliot!" Boog cried. "Aw, disgusting!" Boog's face was shrouded in a stinky cloud as he raced to a stream. Dipping a rabbit in the water, Boog sponged off his reeking body.

Elliot turned away from the stink. He spotted a beautiful doe with delicate features grazing in the meadow. It was a doe from his own herd. His crush!

"It's Giselle!" Elliot said.

"Ridiculous!" Boog muttered, furious. "The woods are no place for a bear!"

Two ducks named Serge and Deni paddled by. When Boog saw the ducks, his eyes lit up. Ducks migrated all the time, so they knew their way around. They also had wings!

"Quick!" Boog said. He lunged toward the ducks. "You guys have got to help me!"

Deni ducked under the water.

"Don't mind Deni, monsieur," Serge said. "He has never been the same since the Great Migration."

Boog stared at Deni's tail, sticking up out of the water. "The what?" he asked.

Serge took a deep breath as he remembered. "There were thousands of us when we flew in the big Vs," he said.

As Serge spoke, Boog could almost see the flocks of ducks flying in magnificent V formations across the sky.

"Then it happened," Serge said in a hushed voice.

"What happened?" Boog asked.

Deni popped his head out of the water. He began quacking air-combat sounds: *Tat-tat-tat! Tat-tat-Tat! Pow! Pow! Pow!*

"Open season happened!" Serge declared. Boog pictured the crispy critters going down like flaming fighter planes.

"Just me and Deni are left. How can you make a V with only two ducks, eh? It is a tragedy. A tragedy."

Boog glanced back and saw Elliot. The deer was busily tying a branch to the stub of his missing antler. He had to lose Elliot, or he'd never get home!

"Yeah, right, whatever," Boog said. "But check this out. Can one of you guys fly up there and tell me which way town is?"

"Fly! Fly! Fly!" Deni cried.

"Quiet," Boog hissed to the ducks, "or he'll hear you!"

Chapter Ten

"Psst," Elliot hissed. "Giselle!"

Giselle lifted her head. The honey-colored doe giggled when she saw the pathetic branch tied to Elliot's stump. She batted her blue eyes at him.

"Elliot?" Giselle asked. "Is that you?"

"Hi, gorgeous," Elliot said. "How are you doing?"

Elliot's heart pounded as he swaggered over to Giselle. He'd had a crush on Giselle for as long as he could remember. But Giselle was Ian's girl. And nobody messed with Ian, the herd's strapping alpha buck.

"Elliot!" Giselle whispered. "Where have you been?"

"Oh, you know, the big city," Elliot said coolly. "Kind of a road trip. Saw the sights, hit the buffet, took in a show. Things are looking up, Giselle."

"Really," Giselle said. "I heard you got hit by a truck."

Busted!

Elliot's branch sagged over his face. "That's just a rumor," he muttered.

Giselle's eyes darted left. Then right.

"You'd better get out of here," Giselle whispered. "You remember what happened the last time you talked to me!"

"Oh!" Elliot gulped. "Is Ian around?"

One of Giselle's eyes winked rapidly.

"How long have you had that tic?" Elliot asked.

Giselle jerked her head toward the field of grass.

"You'd better get that checked," Elliot said. "I think it's getting worse."

Things were about to get worse for Elliot as thirty brawny deer rose from the tall grass.

"Oh, crud," Elliot muttered. So that's what Giselle was trying to tell him!

Elliot froze as Ian lumbered over. The big lug hadn't changed a bit since he almost made deer-patties out of him.

"Hello, Smelliot!" Ian joked. He turned to his herd and laughed. "Hey, I called him Smelliot! Ha, ha, ha!"

"Ha, ha, ha!" The herd laughed along.

Ian stopped laughing. He puffed out his massive chest and shouted, "Herd! Circle formation!"

In a flash the bucks surrounded Elliot.

"You pinheads!" Ian shouted. "That's an oval. More . . . uh . . . circle-y!"

The herd tightened into a perfect circle. Elliot stared up at Ian. His antlers were so huge they blotted out the sun.

"You've got a lot of nerve coming back here," Ian growled.

"Why, thank you," Elliot said.

"That was not a compliment, maggot!" Ian snapped.

"He was just going," Giselle piped in. "Right, Elliot?"

"Yeah, Ian. But I had to stop by and say hello to some of my old pals," Elliot said. He turned to the other guys and grinned. "Bob, Kevin, Jurgen— how's the knee?"

Ian narrowed his eyes. "I told you to leave the

herd and never, ever, ever come back!" he said.

"Back?" Elliot said. "I'm not back." Elliot looked proudly in the direction he had left Boog. "Me and my best buddy are heading to town!" Elliot grinned as he gave Ian's chest a pat. "I'm sure going to miss you guys," he said.

"Off the upholstery!" Ian shouted. Then he scooped his mighty antlers and—*crack*—threw Elliot high into the sky!

"*Aieeeeeee!*" Elliot shrieked.

Boog and the ducks heard the scream.

"What now?" Boog wondered aloud. He raced to the meadow just in time to see Elliot crashing down at Ian's feet.

For the first time in days Boog felt sorry for the scrawny mule deer. Sure, Elliot was a pain in the tail, but in this strange and vast forest, Boog realized Elliot was the only friend he had.

"So as I was saying," Ian went on. "Never, ever—"

"Roooorrrr!" Boog growled.

The bucks parted as Boog charged into the circle. "Bear. Bear!" Ian squeaked.

Elliot watched, punch-drunk, as the herd stepped back. Boog really had them fooled! He actually had them thinking he was a ferocious grizzly bear. What a guy!

"Elliot," Boog said. "Are you all right?"

"Buttermilk biscuit," Elliot mumbled.

A buck behind Boog noticed something strange on Boog's back and tilted his head as he checked out Dinkelman. He began plucking at the teddy bear backpack with his teeth.

"Hey, Ian!" he shouted. "Get a load of this!"

"Cut it out!" Boog ordered. As he whirled around, Ian spotted the cuddly little teddy.

"Hey, I've heard of you!" Ian chuckled. "You're the bear that got your butt thumped by a squirrel. Ha! Ha! Ha!"

"There were twenty of them!" Boog blurted.

Ian, taunting, said, "Ooooh!"

"And they had nuts!"

The herd cracked up laughing.

"Don't listen to them, Boog!" Elliot said, still a little woozy from his crash landing.

"Boog?" Ian guffawed. "What's that short for? Booger?"

The bucks laughed louder. It was more than Boog could take.

"Listen, you—" Boog began to say.

Ian stepped up to Boog's face and said, "I'm all ears!"

Boog's knees turned to jelly. He wasn't a fighting bear, he was a show bear.

"Boog," Elliot said, tugging his arm. "Let's go."

The two tried to leave, but Ian's enormous rack kept getting in the way.

"You two are perfect for each other. You're a loser, and you're a loser-er," Ian sneered.

Before Ian ran off, he twanged Elliot's antler stump with his teeth. "Hey, Elliot," he guffawed, "I think you lost something! Ha! Haa! Haaaa!"

Giselle turned to Elliot and smiled. "Maybe it'll grow back," she said. "Bye, Elliot."

"Yeah, see you." Elliot sighed.

"See you later, backpack boy!" Ian shouted back to Boog. "Herd, let's bound!"

Boog and Elliot waited until the herd was completely out of sight.

"That's right, fool!" Boog called, knowing no one could hear. "Keep on running, you panty-waisted cow!"

"Yeah!" Elliot said toughly. "One more word and I was going to rack him!"

"That's right!" Boog said.

The two patted each other on the back.

"I was waiting for it!" Elliot said. "He's scared. Look at him run! Look at him run!"

Suddenly, a voice called out, "Aren't you gonna buy him a drink before you kiss him?" Then—*whack! Whack!*

Two acorns whizzed out, hitting Boog and Elliot.

They glanced up and groaned. McSquizzy and the Furry Tail Clan were laughing it up from a nearby tree!

Boog and Elliot left the field under a hail of acorns. But this time they left as *buddies*.

Chapter Eleven

"That was Ian's girl you were trying to talk to, right?" Boog asked.

Elliot wearily nodded yes. Night had fallen in the forest and the two travelers knew they would not make it home that night since they had been walking around in circles all day. They plopped down in the tall grass.

"Ian's right." Elliot sighed. "I'm nothing but a loser."

"No," Boog said. "You're not a loser."

"Yes, I am!" Elliot insisted.

"No, you're not!" Boog said.

"Trust me," Elliot said, pointing to his missing antler. "The day I met you, Ian kicked me out of the herd. I got run over, lost my antler, and got tied to the hood of a truck. What do you call that?"

Boog thought about it. All that in one day was pretty lame. So he nodded and agreed, "A loser."

As Elliot gazed at the sky, Boog joined the pity party. He stood up and spread his arms wide.

"Behold the mighty grizzly," Boog scoffed. "I may look like a bear. But I can't fish, I can't climb a tree, I can't even do my business in the woods!"

"That's nothing," Elliot said, pointing to his missing antler. "I'm half doe, half buck! I'm a duck!"

"Hey, I ride a unicycle for crackers!" Boog challenged.

Elliot tried to top it by saying, "Well, I killed a man!" and they both just had to laugh. Until Elliot said, "At least you have a home."

Boog's heart ached as he remembered his garage apartment and Beth. Did Beth still love him? Would he ever be able to go home again? Boog slipped Dinkelman off his back and fluffed him up like a pillow.

"Home," Boog said. "I sure hope so."

As Boog rested his head on Dinkelman, he heard a loud *crunch*!

"Was that your neck?" Elliot gasped.

"No," Boog said. He sat up and unzipped Dinkelman. He looked inside and grinned. Beth had stuffed his backpack with his favorite fishy crackers!

"She still loves me!" Boog cried. "Thank you, Beth! I'm coming home! I'm coming home!"

Boog popped a yummy cracker into his mouth. Then he handed one to Elliot.

"Try one, partner," Boog said. "They're not Woo-Hoo bars, but they remind me of my home. Sweet, salty home!"

Elliot popped a cracker into his mouth. He crunched on it for awhile and—

"Bleeeeech!"

As Elliot spit out cracker crumbs, Boog got comfortable on the grass.

"To be back in my own soft bed," Boog said. "Eight square meals a day plus snacks. Beth tucking me in every night. Sounds like heaven to me!"

Elliot's one good antler drooped as he watched a smile spread across Boog's dreamy face. What would become of their friendship if Boog went home? What would become of Boogster and the Incredible Mister E? And what would become of their show?

"When we get back home tomorrow, I'm going to make things right with Beth," Boog rambled on. "And maybe—just maybe—we can find a place for you in the garage, too."

Elliot brightened.

"Sweet!" Elliot said. He kicked up his hooves and began dancing around. "Who's staying in the garage? I'm in the garage! Who's got a place in the garage? That's me! Oh, yeah! Oh, yeah!"

"Hey, buddy?" Boog asked.

Elliot stopped dancing. "Yeah?"

"This is going to sound silly," Boog said. "But . . . can you sing me a lullaby?"

Elliot smiled. Anything for his buddy!

"Absolutely!" Elliot said. "Um . . . what song?"

"Dinkelman plays the music," Boog explained. "It helps me to fall asleep."

"Okay," Elliot said. "I'll give it a shot." Elliot didn't exactly know the song, but for a warm cozy place in the garage he would sing upside down on his one antler with a mouth full of fishy crackers!

Boog tugged the string on Dinkelman's back. The plunkety little tune began to play.

Elliot cleared his throat. He began to sing, making up the words as he went along . . .

"Once there was a magical elf who lived in a rainbow tree. He lived downstairs from a flatulent dwarf who was constantly having to pee. One day the elf could take no more so he went and banged on the rude dwarf's door . . . and what do you know they suddenly both were married."

While Boog began to snore, Elliot danced again.

"I'm sleeping in the garage!" he sang. "I'm sleeping in the garage!"

Elliot fell down on the grass next to Boog. He had never been so happy. Finally his life had purpose and he would have a home.

Not too far away, a human couple, Bob and Bobbie, sat around a blazing campfire with their beloved little dachshund, Mr. Weenie.

84

"Come on, Mr. Weenie!" Bobbie urged. She held a marshmallow on a stick out to the little dog. "You can do it. Beg! Beg!"

Mr. Weenie sat on a log, wearing his newly knitted striped doggy sweater. His owners were far-out, crunchy-granola types, always into something new. Like dressing their dog and teaching him tricks for marshmallows.

"He won't listen, Bob!" Bobbie said. "Let's show him how to do it!"

"Okay," Bob said.

The two kneeled in front of Mr. Weenie. They raised their "paws" and began to pant.

Mr. Weenie hardly noticed. But somebody watching in the woods did. . . .

"Aaaaahh!" Shaw cried. He screeched his truck to a stop when he saw Bob and Bobbie begging at an animal's feet.

Looking closer, Shaw frowned. He had seen that animal once before—it was the same little dog that he'd seen driving the camper on the road!

Shaw climbed out of his truck. He crept toward the campfire and peeked out from behind a tree.

"Dog worship!" Shaw hissed. It was the end of civilization as they knew it, unless he could save the day!

Shaw sounded a battle cry as he broke through the trees. He tackled Mr. Weenie and held him in a headlock.

"Oh, my goodness! Oh, my goodness!" Bobbie cried. "What are you doing?"

Chapter Twelve

"You folks all right?" Shaw asked.

Mr. Weenie yelped under Shaw's steely grip.

"What?" Bobbie cried. "You don't understand. He's—"

"—taken you hostage!" Shaw cut in. "But don't worry, because you're safe now. I've got the enemy under control!"

Mr. Weenie stared up at Shaw. Then he stretched out his fat little neck and bit him right on the nose!

"Owwww!" Shaw yelled.

Mr. Weenie broke free. He jumped into Bobbie's arms to a shower of kisses.

"There, there, Mr. Weenie," Bobbie cooed. "Are you all right, baby?"

"Don't be fooled," Shaw said, rubbing his nose. "He's one of them."

"One of who?" Bobbie asked.

"The enemy! That bear! That deer!" Shaw shouted. "All of them! *Animals!* You can't trust them!"

Shaw leaned closer to Bob and Bobbie. "I have seen the future," he said in a hushed voice, sharing his vision. "It will start in small towns like Timberline, but soon it will spread. They'll invade from burrows, caves, and petting zoos!"

Bob and Bobbie listened to Shaw's theory with wide eyes. They pictured animals driving cars down Main Street. Animals leading humans on leashes. Animals out of control!

"If I don't stop them, it'll be a total reversal of the natural order," Shaw said. "They laugh at old Shaw, but soon you'll see. The truth will prevail."

Bob and Bobbie both smiled.

"Oh, we know what you mean," Bobbie rambled. "We're scientists of sorts, and we're trying to secure photographic documentation of a real, live Homo sasquatchus!"

"Homo-say-whatsus?" Shaw asked.

"We're looking for Bigfoot," Bobbie explained.

Shaw hadn't realized he was dealing with

a bunch of wackos. He grabbed a marshmallow on a stick and pointed it at Mr. Weenie. "Don't trust him," he warned. "Pets are double agents!"

He bit off the marshmallow and trudged into the woods. Bob and Bobbie stared at their little Mr. Weenie. No way would he ever turn against them.

He never learned that trick, either!

"Boog? Boog?" Elliot whispered. "Are you awake?"

It was the crack of dawn and Boog was still snoring like a buzz saw. Elliot sat on Boog's chest. He pried one eyelid open.

"I am now," Boog said.

Elliot jumped off Boog.

"Awesome!" he said. "I was watching you sleep last night and you were like an angel. Except for your snoring. But I invented a cure for that!"

Elliot shoved his whole hoof in his mouth then took it out again. "See?" he said. "Stick your hand in your mouth!"

Boog didn't care about his snoring problem. All he cared about was getting home to Beth.

"How long to Timberline?" Boog asked.

"By nightfall," Elliot answered.

"Then we'd better get going," Boog said.

Elliot grabbed Dinkelman and said, "Right. We're on a tight schedule."

Boog stared at Elliot holding Dinkelman. Nobody ever carried Dinkelman but him!

"L-look," Boog stammered. "You have to be real careful with him. He's very delicate."

Elliot unzipped Dinkelman and reached inside. "Want a fishy cracker?" he asked.

"No, thanks." Boog sighed. "I'll eat when I get home."

The two buddies continued their journey. As they passed two bickering skunks in the woods, Boog remembered the cloud of stink. He had a feeling he had seen and smelled those two before.

"Hey," Boog said slowly. "Aren't those the same skunks we saw yesterday?"

Elliot wasn't paying attention to his surroundings. His mind was on more important things.

"I had some thoughts on the show," Elliot said.

"Whoa!" Boog cried. "You mean *my* show?"

"The lady in the shorts has got to go," Elliot decided. "She's slowing us down. It's going to be fresh and new. I want to jazz it up!"

Boog couldn't believe it. Moving into his garage wasn't enough for Elliot? Now he had to take over his show?

"In case you're forgetting, I'm the star!" Boog said. "People come from all over to see me. A grizzly bear!"

Elliot's mouth became a grim line. "Oh, I see," he said. "You get to have a career while I stay home and look after Dinkelman."

Elliot dropped Dinkelman on the ground. He leaned against a tree and sulked. "I don't get to have a dream, is that it?" Elliot asked. "Don't you think I might like a little singing? A little dancing? A little cha, cha, chaaaa?"

Boog caught a glimpse of a beaver dam through some bushes. It looked like the same beaver dam from yesterday!

"Elliot?" Boog asked.

"But no," Elliot went on. "All I ever hear is, 'How long until we get home? How long until we get to Timberline?'"

"Elliot!" Boog shouted. He grabbed Elliot by his antler and swung him around. "Aren't those the same beavers over there?"

"No," Elliot said. "All beavers look alike."

But when the beavers saw Boog, they went wild.

"Hey, Tiny Dancer!" Reilly said. He swiveled his hips back and forth. "Let's see some moves!"

"Yeah, that's right!" O'Toole laughed. "Shake it, baby! Shake it!"

Boog scowled as the beavers shook it up. They were the same beavers, all right. And the skunks were the same skunks.

"Elliot!" Boog screamed. "We've been going around in circles!"

"Circle," Elliot corrected. "One time around."

"Aaaarrrgh!" Boog screamed. "I am so tired of your talk, talk, talk—"

Blam!

The animals froze as a gunshot exploded behind them. Though they couldn't actually see Shaw standing on top of the hill, they had a pretty good idea who had fired the shot.

"Hunters!" O'Toole cried. "What are they doing up here?"

As boss beaver, Reilly sprung into action.

"Take cover, boys!" he ordered.

One by one, the beavers jumped off the dam.

"Boog, we've got to hide!" Elliot said.

Boog was freaking out, too. He dropped Elliot, picked up Dinkelman, and began to run.

"I'm out of here!" Boog said.

Elliot shot after Boog as he raced across the dam. "Boog, don't go out there! It's dangerous!" he called.

"Whoa, tubby!" Reilly shouted to Boog. "This is not a load-bearing structure!"

Boog kept on running. Until—*snap*—a twig on the dam broke. Tiny leaks along the dam spurted water as it began to give way.

"Uh-oh," Elliot said. "That's bad."

Boog glared at Elliot. If it wasn't for his lame directions they wouldn't be lost in the first place. He reached out to grab Elliot's scrawny neck—when the entire dam collapsed like a pile of popsicle sticks!

"Aaaaahh!" Boog and Elliot screamed.

They were crashing down with the dam, into the raging waters below!

Chapter
Thirteen

Boog was still screaming as the two smashed into a floating log. Sitting inside the log were Rosie and Maria, the two sassy skunks.

The log rode the powerful currents like an out-of-control roller coaster. A whimpering Elliot clung to Boog's head.

"Stop!" Boog shouted. "Get off of me!"

"Buuuuuudeeeee!" a tiny voice called.

Elliot saw a little porcupine standing in the middle of the stream. It was the same porcupine who had been stuck on Boog's butt. Now he was stuck on a rock as the waters raged around him.

"Uh-oh," Elliot said.

The porcupine took a flying leap. Elliot screamed as needle-sharp quills pierced his face.

All of the animals screamed as they tumbled off the log into the angry waters.

While the animals paddled for their lives, Shaw drove up the dry riverbed. He screeched to a stop when he saw a wall of water racing toward him. The powerful wave smashed into his truck and carried it down the river.

Shaw looked out his windshield and gulped. He was underwater. But instead of seeing fish, he saw a beaver, a skunk—and Boog and Elliot floating by!

"Wha—?" Shaw gulped.

"Shhhhhaaawwwww!" Elliot gurgled.

Boog clutched Dinkelman as he rode the currents, but they were so strong they ripped Dinkelman from his arms.

"Dinkelman!" Boog gurgled.

Boog began to go under, but then he felt someone pull him to the surface. It was Elliot, riding on another floating log.

"You're going to be okay, Boog," Elliot said.

Just when they thought they were safe, Shaw's truck breached the surface of the water like a giant whale.

"Ha, ha, ha!" Shaw laughed.

Boog and Elliot paddled the log away from him. But Shaw gunned his engine and the truck surged forward after them.

"No one is around here to save you this time, boys!" Shaw shouted from the window of his truck.

Elliot looked back. Shaw was gaining on them!

"Paddle, Boog! Paddle!" Elliot cried.

Both animals paddled furiously until they heard the sound of rushing waters.

"We're heading for the rapids!" Elliot cried.

"Grab a boulder, Elliot!" Boog shouted. "Grab a boulder!"

Their log bounced through the rapids. Elliot tried to grab a boulder, but they were going too fast!

Shaw laughed as he watched from his truck. He stopped laughing when his truck hit a boulder and shot through the air.

"Whoooaaaa!" Shaw screamed.

"Where'd he go?" Boog asked.

Elliot glanced back. Shaw's truck was no longer on their trail.

"He's gone!" Elliot declared.

Shaw's truck reappeared on the water behind them.

"There he is!" Elliot shouted.

The truck bobbed in and out of the water like a wet and wild whack-a-mole game.

"There he is!" Elliot said, pointing. "No—there he is. No—there he is—"

"Quiet!" Boog shouted. "I'm trying to drive!"

Shaw peered at the animals through his windshield. He grabbed his rifle and climbed out the window of his truck.

When Boog and Elliot looked back, they saw Shaw standing on the roof of his truck. He was aiming his gun straight at them.

"Aaaaahh!" they shouted.

A shot rang out. Instead of hitting the animals, the bullet hit a rock.

"Missed!" Shaw muttered.

But he was not about to give up. When the three reached the end of the rapids, he reloaded his gun and fired again.

Bram! This time Shaw hit the water.

Missed again!

"Faster, Boog! Faster!" Elliot cried.

Shaw sneered as Boog paddled the log through the now calmer waters. Maybe he would get them in the next shot!

He picked up his gun and zeroed in on Boog and Elliot. Chasing animals on the river was like hunting and fishing at the same time.

Shaw grinned as he saw Boog and Elliot in the gun scope. Closer . . . closer . . . he really had those two now!

Until the log suddenly disappeared.

"Where did they go?" Shaw asked himself.

He peeked over his gun. When he saw what was up ahead, his heart sank. His truck was speeding straight toward the edge of a giant waterfall!

Chapter Fourteen

Boog and Elliot clung to their log as it sped down the face of the gushing waterfall. As they took the plunge, they argued all the way down.

"Give me a hand, Boog!" Elliot shouted.

"Stop it!" Boog shouted back. "Get off of me!"

"Come on, Boog, share!" Elliot cried.

"Elliot—I said get off of me—stop!" Boog said.

The animals turned their heads and screamed. Falling right next to them was Shaw. He whipped out his rifle and aimed again.

"Ha, ha, ha!" Shaw laughed.

Boog saw his whole life flash before him. The first part was fabulous. The last part he'd rather forget.

Shaw pulled the trigger. But instead of hearing a shot he heard a *click*.

His beloved rifle, Lorraine, was empty!

Boog and Elliot traded hopeful looks. But Shaw was already reloading his gun in midair. He was just about to fire when the falls crashed down on the valley floor.

The waters hit a rabbit warren. Hundreds of surprised rabbits popped out of their holes. They hung in midair on gushing geysers.

As the floodwaters dropped, Boog and Elliot lay on the bank. They looked and felt like two drowned rats!

Sitting up, Boog and Elliot watched Shaw's truck float by. They sighed as it slowly sank in the water.

As he shook the water off of his fur, Boog spotted something sticking out of the ground. It was coated with mud but looked soft and plush.

"Dinkelman?" Boog gasped.

He yanked the object out of the ground, but after he'd shaken the mud off he sighed. It wasn't Dinkelman at all. Just another rabbit.

Boog looked out over the mud-filled valley and all the animals he and Elliot had met up the river.

They too were drenched, dazed, and confused!

"You!" Reilly shouted. He pointed an accusing paw at Boog. "You did this!"

"What?" Boog asked. "What did I do?"

"You've dragged us down to the hunting grounds!" Reilly said. The water had ruined their homes; they had no place to go and hunting season was starting. The animals blamed it all on Boog.

The animals began circling the bear.

"Where are we going to hide now?" Maria demanded.

"We are sitting ducks out here!" Serge cried.

"And it's open season!" the porcupine called from the tree he was stuck on.

Boog wasn't used to being so hated. He was used to being loved by Beth and his adoring fans. How did things get so warped?

Elliot broke through the hostile crowd. He grabbed Boog's arm and said, "All right, that's enough. It's not his fault, you guys."

Boog yanked his arm back. "That's right. It's not my fault. It's *your* fault!"

"My fault?" Elliot asked.

"Yeah!" Boog said. "If it weren't for you, I'd be home right now. None of this ever would have happened. You said you knew the way back home, but you lied!"

It was time to get real. Elliot shrugged his scrawny shoulders and said, "I thought if you hung out with me long enough, you'd start to like me."

Boog couldn't believe his waterlogged ears.

Elliot got them lost on purpose!

"Man, I trusted you, Elliot!" Boog said.

"I'm sorry, Boog," Elliot said. "We're still partners, right?"

"You know, Elliot," Boog said, "I think I'm better off alone!"

"What about us?" the porcupine called.

"Us?! There is no *us*!" Boog said. He turned angrily to Elliot. "As for you, we're done!"

The words hit Elliot like a ton of Woo-Hoo bars. His heart sank as his only buddy in the world walked away.

"Boog, wait!" Elliot called.

"Done!" Boog repeated.

He stomped his way into the forest. As he walked deeper and deeper into the woods, rain began to fall. A clap of thunder made Boog jump. Maybe leaving Elliot wasn't such a good idea. . . .

Boog shook his head. Leaving Elliot was the best idea he'd had so far. He never cared about that ditzy deer anyway. All he cared about was getting back to Timberline and to Beth. And, most of all, back to the way things used to be!

Chapter Fifteen

Beth stood alone on the stage. The theater seats were empty and so was her heart. She sighed as she packed the last traces of Boog into a big cardboard box. Beth picked up a framed picture that had been taken just after she had rescued the bear cub. In it, she was holding the recently orphaned baby bear in her arms.

Beth added the picture to the other memories. She picked up the box with one hand and dragged Boog's squeaky unicycle with the other. She left the theater and trudged to the parking lot. As Beth loaded her jeep, she heard a jingling noise. Turning around she saw Gordy chaining a new sign to the door of the Fish and Game office: OPEN SEASON: *TODAY!*

The door of the office slammed open and a hunter walked out. He was smiling from ear to ear as he held up a piece of paper.

"Thanks for the hunting license, Gordy!" he said.

"Sure," Gordy replied. "Good luck!"

"Okay, boys!" the hunter shouted. "We're legal! Let's get going!"

The other hunters whooped and hollered. Beth felt sick as the hunters climbed into their trucks and fired up their engines. All she could think about was Boog.

"Are you okay, Beth?" Gordy asked, walking over.

"I know I put Boog way above the falls where it's safe," Beth said slowly. "But I hope I did the right thing."

An angry storm cloud passed over their heads. Gordy put his arm gently around Beth's shoulder.

"Don't worry, Beth," he said. "I'm sure Boog is happy in his new home."

* * *

"Trees! Bushes! Rain!" Boog grumbled as he stomped through the rain-soaked woods. "Stupid nature!"

Boog had no clue where he was or where he was going. As he sloshed another few feet through the muddy forest, he saw a light in the distance. It was coming from the window of a small cabin. And a cabin meant—

"Civilization!" Boog cried.

Boog ran straight to the cabin. The door creaked as he pulled it open.

"Hello? Anybody home?" Boog called.

He walked inside and looked around. A lamp dangling from the ceiling cast an eerie bluish glow throughout the cabin. Boog spotted another door. He peeked through it and gasped. There, gleaming white in the darkness, was a toilet.

"Oh, sweet porcelain!" Boog cried. No more bushes! No more tree stumps! No more "grr" face!

He ran inside the room and shut the door. After a few minutes Boog emerged victorious. He had done his thing. Now it was time for a little snack!

"There's got to be a fridge around here

somewhere," Boog said. Stumbling around in the dim light, he spotted what he was searching for.

He pulled the handle and the door popped open. When Boog looked inside his eyes lit up. The refrigerator was practically empty except for a wonderful surprise: a candy bar. One whiff of the sweet chocolate bar and Boog was in Woo-Hoo heaven!

Next Boog needed a comfy place to eat and relax. He felt his way through the dark until he found a big, cushy chair against the wall. Boog sighed as he sank deep into it. But when he tugged a chain to turn on the light . . .

"Ohhh!" Boog said. He stared at a tiny stuffed paw on the chain handle. His eyes followed the chain up to a lamp made out of a stuffed rabbit swinging a golf club.

Boog fell back in the chair. The lamp toppled off the table and the light went out.

As Boog sat in the dark, his heart thumped. What demented person would have a stuffed rabbit lamp in his home? A stuffed rabbit that played golf?

Just then something hard landed on Boog's shoulder. He turned his head and screamed. Perched on his shoulder was a big stuffed deer head—with glass eyes!

Boog jumped out of the chair. A flash of lightning lit up the cabin and revealed dozens of stuffed animal heads hanging on the wall. Terrified, Boog looked from one head to the next until his eyes landed on the head of a bear.

Boog's paws flew up to his neck. He sighed with relief when he felt his head still there. He was looking into a mirror!

But Boog's relief didn't last for long.

He stared at the poor grimacing souls on the wall. This place was no cozy little cabin in the woods. It was a house of horrors!

Suddenly he heard a *click!* The handle on the front door creaked as it turned slowly.

"Oh, no." Boog gulped.

Someone was coming!

Chapter Sixteen

"Deers, skunks, beavers," Shaw muttered as he entered his cabin. "That bear's turned them all!"

Boog took one look at Shaw and backed against the wall. He should have known the cabin belonged to him. He had to hide!

Boog was too big to squeeze behind the pot-bellied stove or fake being a bearskin rug. He jumped straight up and dug his claws into the rafters. Boog hung there as Shaw plopped the beloved Dinkelman on a table. After pouring rainwater out of his gun barrel, Shaw struck a match and lit the stove. He then wrapped his gun in a blanket and placed it lovingly on a rocking chair in front of the stove.

"There you go, Lorraine," Shaw said. "You get

good and dry. Because tomorrow we've got a rebellion to crush."

Shaw reached inside his vest and pulled out an antler. He held it up and with confidence declared, "Then I'm going to take back what's mine!"

Boog gulped as Shaw stabbed the antler into an empty plaque on the wall.

"Elliot!" Boog whispered.

He felt his claws lose their grip. As Shaw moved to the refrigerator, Boog dropped to the floor.

Shaw looked inside the refrigerator.

"Someone's been eating my candy!" he said.

Boog had to get out of there and fast! He scrambled under a table just as Shaw walked across the room to the broken chair.

"Somebody's been sitting in my chair!" Shaw said.

He entered the bathroom and took a whiff.

"And somebody forgot to flush!" Shaw said.

Boog held his breath as he stood behind Shaw. He saw Dinkelman on the table and reached out to grab him. The minute Boog touched the teddy bear, music began to play!

In a panic Boog pulled his paw back. Then—

Ploing! Shaw's hunting knife stabbed the table between Boog's paw and Dinkelman.

"And he's still here!" Shaw growled.

Boog's blood turned to ice. He dove under the table just as Shaw ripped an axe from the wall.

"Come back for your bear, Goldilocks?" Shaw called. "Ready or not, here I come!"

But when Shaw flipped the table over, he shrieked. Boog was gone. All that was on the floor was a trapdoor leading to the root cellar.

Shaw opened the door and climbed into the cellar. Boog trembled behind hanging animal pelts as he listened to Shaw singing Boog's favorite song. . . .

Boog shuddered. Only a monster like Shaw could make his favorite tune sound so sinister.

Shaw laughed. He stabbed his knife into a pelt and ripped it in half. He didn't see Boog, but he did hear him thundering up the cellar stairs.

"Huh?" Shaw said.

Upstairs Boog wasted no time. He grabbed Shaw's shotgun off the rocking chair. He rammed it between the trapdoor handles. Then Boog darted out the front door and ran for his life.

Shaw smashed against the cellar door until the handles ripped apart. Picking up his rifle, he bolted out the front door after Boog.

"Hey, bear!" Shaw shouted as he cocked his gun. "Ain't nowhere that you can hide from me now!"

But Boog was nowhere in sight. He was already deep in the forest, smashing through the brush and crashing through the trees.

Boog's heart pounded faster and faster as he ran from Shaw. He tripped and fell facedown in front of two painted yellow lines.

Boog turned his head just as a hunter's truck barreled straight toward him. He was in the middle of a busy road!

Quickly Boog picked himself up and hid in the bushes. He waited until all the pickup trucks had zoomed by. Then he carefully walked back to the middle of the road.

As Boog gazed down the road, he saw twinkling lights. Were they more headlights?

But as Boog looked closer he smiled. They were the twinkling lights of Timberline!

"Aw!" Boog sighed.

He walked toward his town, then stopped and glanced back. He remembered the hunters' trucks, heading toward the forest to fire the first shots of open season.

Then Boog remembered something else . . .

"Elliot," he said softly.

Chapter Seventeen

"Once there was a magical elf who lived in a rainbow tree," Elliot sang as he trudged through the woods. His whole body was bent with exhaustion as he dragged himself into a clearing. "He lived downstairs—"

"Elliot!" a voice hissed.

"Huh?" Elliot looked up.

It was Giselle, peeking out of a bush.

"You've got to hide, Elliot," Giselle whispered. "The hunters are here."

Elliot looked around. More animals were hiding in the bushes and behind trees: the baby porcupine, Rosie and Maria the skunks, Reilly the boss beaver, even that lug of a buck, Ian.

May as well join the club, Elliot thought. He shimmied into a hollow tree, with his tail waving out of the hole. Elliot's singing voice echoed loudly inside the tree and through the woods.

"Oh!" Reilly said, squirming nervously. "He's going to give us away!"

Elliot heard a twig snap. He felt someone grab his tail and yank him out of the tree trunk. Next thing he knew, he was hanging upside down.

"All right!" Elliot said. "Bring it! Bring it!"

Elliot squeezed his eyes shut. Then he heard a laugh. Opening one eye, Elliot saw an upside-down but familiar face . . .

"Boog?" Elliot asked.

"Hey, buddy," Boog said.

"What are you doing back here?" Elliot asked.

"I couldn't go home without my partner," Boog said with a smile.

"I don't have a partner," Elliot said. "I don't need the herd and I don't need you. So leave me alone."

Still hanging by his tail, Elliot turned his back to Boog.

A wave of sadness swept through Elliot. His herd walked out on him. Boog walked out on him. How could he depend on anyone anymore? From now on it was the single life for him.

"Not going to be able to do it," Boog said. "You see, I already saved you once. So that makes me responsible for you."

"Huh?" Elliot said. Where had he heard those words before? Wait a minute—those were *his* words!

Elliot glanced sideways at Boog. Then he quickly looked away.

"I saw that!" said Boog. "Come on. Let me hear you say it. Partners."

"No," Elliot said.

"What was that?" Boog asked.

Elliot sighed. Who was he kidding? He still wanted a friend. He still wanted a home. "I guess we can be partners," Elliot mumbled.

"I can't hear you!" Boog said.

"I said," Elliot mumbled, "I guess we can be partners."

"P . . . p . . . p . . . " Boog began to say.

"Partners!" Elliot and Boog declared together.

Boog dropped Elliot on the ground. The deer jumped up with a big smile on his face.

"Okeydokey," Elliot said. "This way!"

Boog grabbed Elliot's antler and swung him in

116

the other direction. "This way!" he said.

"Right," Elliot chuckled. "Maybe you'd better lead."

But Boog trembled as he glanced around. The woods were quiet for now. Any minute they would explode with hunters.

"Let's go back to the garage," Boog said, "where it's safe."

Rosie and Maria peered out from behind a tree. Reilly popped up from behind a rock. Giselle peeked out of a bush.

Did he say *safe*?

Boog and Elliot carefully made their way through the woods, sneaking from tree to tree.

"Hey, Boog?" Elliot whispered. "How many animals can fit in the garage?"

"What do you mean?" Boog asked.

He turned around and gasped. Tip-toeing behind them was every animal in the forest!

"Hi, Boog!" the creatures chimed together.

Boog was afraid to ask. But he did anyway. "So . . . where are you all headed?"

"To the safe place!" Giselle said.

"This Land of Garage!" Ian declared.

"With Buddy!" the porcupine piped up.

"Come on, tiny!" Reilly said. "You owe us!"

"Oh, yeah," Boog said. "The dam . . . the flood . . . sorry about your damage and how I messed you all up. My bad."

Pushing his way through the crowd, Ian got right up into Boog's face. "You're taking us with you, right, Booger?" he asked.

Boog didn't answer.

"Please!" Ian sobbed, collapsing in front of Boog's feet. "I'm too pretty to die!"

"Well . . . maybe," Boog said.

Then he imagined his garage packed with animals, rabbits spilling out of windows and the door.

What was he thinking??

"No! No! No!" Boog screamed.

The animals rushed toward Boog.

"You're not leaving without us!" Rosie cried.

"You got us into this mess!" Maria snapped.

"I didn't mean to call you Booger!" Ian sobbed.

"Hey, buddy?" Elliot asked. "Can we take Giselle?"

Boog's head was spinning. He had agreed to take in Elliot, not every woodland creature in the entire forest!

Then again, how could he leave the animals to be hunted down?

"Stop!" Boog shouted. "Let me think!"

Boog stepped away from the panicky crowd. He kept stepping back, back, and back until he saw something that stopped him dead in his tracks.

"Huh?" Boog said.

Their only way home was lined with countless flickering campfires. Hunters' campfires. The animals stared at the campsites with wide, terrified eyes.

"Nobody is going home tonight," Boog said quietly.

They were trapped.

Chapter Eighteen

"There are so many of them," Reilly said.

"I guess that's it, then." Giselle sighed.

"No more . . . me," the porcupine gulped.

"I'll probably be mounted on a wall," Elliot cried.

Boog shook his head. He put on his "grr" face and said, "No, you won't. When I'm a bearskin rug, they can walk all over me. Until that happens, I'm not going out without a fight!"

The animals stared at Boog.

He just said the "F" word: *Fight!*

"That's right!" Boog said. "If there's one thing you have all taught me, it is that the forest is a messed up, dangerous place."

He looked at the animals and added, "And you're all crazy. You've been busting my chops for the last two days."

The creatures traded embarrassed looks. They had to admit they hadn't been too easy on Boog. But life in the woods wasn't that easy, either!

"I say we do to them what you've been doing to me!" Boog declared. "Let's give our guests the full outdoor experience!"

"I'll give it a shot!" Ian said.

"For sure!" Serge said. *"Quack. Quack."*

Out of nowhere an acorn shot out, hitting Boog with a *ponk*.

"Ow!" Boog said, rubbing his head.

McSquizzy and his bushy-tailed soldiers popped out of the trees.

"Is this a private fight?" McSquizzy shouted. "Or can anyone join? Because McSquizzy wants in!"

"Oi!" shouted the Furry Tail Clan.

Boog smiled at the squirrels. If they were going to take on those nasty hunters, they were going to need all the help they could get.

"Good!" Boog said. "We'll need your nuts."

The animals formed a huddle. They were ready to rumble!

"What's the plan, Boog?" Giselle murmured.

"We're going to round up those yahoos and run

them back to town," Boog said. "When we get through with them, they won't ever come back!"

The odd were about to get even!

The animals moved quietly toward a camper that was unoccupied. After making sure no humans were around, they had a field day ransacking the campsite for supplies.

"Oh, yeah!" Reilly said, grabbing a chain saw.

They snatched clothes from a clothesline, pots and pans, spoons and forks. Rosie and Maria fought over a bag of marshmallows. Rosie won the tug-of-war, but when she looked inside she frowned. "Aw," she said. "It's empty!"

"Ladies," the porcupine said. He walked by with marshmallows stuck to his quills. So that's where they went!

"This is going to be great!" McSquizzy said as he snatched a propane tank from the camper.

The ducks Serge and Deni made two golf clubs their weapons of choice. Elliot got lucky, too—he found a cooler stashed with Woo-Hoo bars.

"Woo-hoooo!" Elliot shouted.

The four-legged army lugged their loot as they

tip-toed away. Suddenly out of the shadows jumped a tiny hot-dog-shaped creature with a pointed nose and floppy ears. It was Mr. Weenie— protector of the campsite!

"Grrr," Mr. Weenie growled.

His owners, Bob and Bobbie, had gone off to gaze at the moon. Now all the animals were gazing at Mr. Weenie. With his little striped doggy sweater, he was definitely not one of them.

"Whoa!" Boog cried.

"It's a pet!" the porcupine cried.

"He's going to blow our cover!" Reilly complained.

Then Mr. Weenie did something that surprised everybody. He stood on his hind legs and ripped off his sweater.

"I have been living a lie!" Mr. Weenie shouted. "Please take me with you!"

The army had one more recruit as Mr. Weenie fell in line with the others. Boog kept up the morale as they crossed a log bridge in front of a waterfall.

"You're doing great, keep it moving," Boog said. He turned to Serge and Deni. "We're going to need more ducks."

Serge and Deni used their wings to salute, then they took off to find another flock.

The ragtag army reached the other side of the bridge. There they constructed a giant slingshot using a buck's antlers and underwear from the clothesline. Boog recognized the other buck, who was resting in the slingshot. It was the same bully who had teased him about Dinkelman.

"Hey, Boog." The buck chuckled. "You're not still mad about that backpack thing, are you?"

"No," Boog said. "I just let it go. I don't hold a grudge."

Boog narrowed his eyes. He stretched back the slingshot and—*thwang*—sent the buck flying and screaming through the air.

Two hunters in the distance watched the soaring buck. What was that?

While they wondered and scratched their heads, Serge and Deni planned their attack. Holding Rosie and Maria in their bills, the ducks glided over the forest.

"Okay, Deni!" Serge said. "Let's round them up."

In a flash, the sky was filled with squadrons of ducks armed with skunks.

"All right, ladies!" Maria shouted. "Let 'em rip!"

As the skunks flew over the forest, they released clouds of stink over the unsuspecting campsites. Hunters ran out from behind trees and bushes, choking and gasping for air.

"Gas masks!" Boog told his troop.

"Got it!" Reilly said.

With rabbits covering their noses, the beavers raced into the tall grass.

"Aaaaahh!" one hunter yelled. "My pants!"

The hunter screamed and yelped as he grabbed at his pants. Boog watched as Reilly and the beaver brigade shot back out of the grass—with armloads of polka-dotted and striped boxer shorts they had ripped off the hunters.

"All right!" Boog shouted. "It's time to run these guys back to town!"

"Let's do it!" Reilly cheered.

A militia of sturdy deer marched out on the ridge. Elliot was perched on Ian's back. "This is awkward, isn't it?" commented Elliot. "Very." Ian sighed. But it was clear that the two of them had buried the hatchet.

"Chaaaaaarge!" Elliot shouted.

The herd thundered off the ridge toward the meadow below. The surprised hunters shrieked when they saw the deer charge through the thick cloud of skunk spray.

"It's a stampede!"

Chapter Nineteen

"All right, troops!" Boog shouted. "Show me your 'grr' face!"

"Grrrrr!"

Boog held up a toilet plunger and a metal shield. "Now let's kick some hunter bahookie!" he said.

The animals pulled up their own shields. They began to move out.

"Come on, mate!" McSquizzy said on the back of Mr. Weenie. "Move them pudgy wee legs!"

Mr. Weenie let out a howl of joy. "I feel so alive!" he said.

As for Elliot, he felt in control as he led his army of bucks. "Drop antlers!" he ordered.

The deer herd lowered their heads. They crashed into the mass of hunters just as Boog and his troops attacked from the other side.

"Out of my way!" the animals shouted.

"Let's get 'em!"

The battle raged.

Unsuspecting hunters were attacked with spoons and porcupine quills. Animals blasted the hunters with canned cheese spray.

"How are you doing, partner?" Boog asked.

"This is great, Boog," Elliot said. "Let's do this every year."

But not all of the animals were victorious. The little porcupine found himself trapped and staring into the barrel of a hunter's rifle.

"Gotcha!" the hunter said.

Giselle bounded over. With a swing of her hoof she kicked the hunter in the gut. "Hee-yaaaa!" she shouted.

Nearby hunters aimed their guns at a group of terrified rabbits. The rabbits thought they were doomed until they glanced up and saw the Furry Tail Clan.

"Fire!" the squirrels shouted.

The hunters yelped as the squirrels pelted them with nuts and cooking utensils.

"Let's get out of here!"

The hunters raced across the log bridge. They had no idea that Reilly stood underneath, buzzing away with his chain saw. Reilly grinned as the log began to split, dumping the screaming hunters into the stream below. As the hunters hit the water, they were greeted by more creatures— the Kung Fu Fighting Salmon!

One hunter on dry land called for help on his cell phone: "Sheriff, the animals have gone wild!" he cried. "And the bear is their leader—"

His call was cut short when he was jumped by a gang of rabbits. As the hunter went down, he snapped a picture with his camera phone. It made its way straight to Sheriff Gordy.

"It's for you, Beth," Gordy said, passing his own camera phone to her.

Beth stared at the picture on the tiny screen. It was her Boog—running amuck through the fields with a toilet plunger.

"Gordy!" Beth gasped. "I'm bringing Boog home!"

Chapter Twenty

The hunters were down but not out. They had come to the forest to hunt, not to be hunted!

"Come on, men!" one hunter declared. "They're just animals!"

Boog heard the battle cry. He could see the hunters charging with their weapons. From his foraged camping gear Boog pulled out a safety flare. He lit it and tossed it to Elliot.

"Got it!" Elliot said.

The buck brigade fell into line, underwear stretched across their antlers. McSquizzy and the Furry Tail Clan rode their backs. They held marshmallows speared on long barbecue forks.

Elliot sat on Ian's back. He made his way down the line of deer, lighting marshmallows with the flare.

"Yyyyyaaaaa!" Elliot cried.

The Furry Tail Clan heeded the battle cry. They loaded the fork handles into the undies and stretched them all the way back.

"Fire!" Boog shouted.

The squirrels snapped the undies, launching the marshmallows into the air. The hunters stopped charging when they saw the flaming hail of marshmallows.

"Back to the trucks!" they shouted.

The animals cheered as the hunters ran for their lives. Their plan of attack was working!

"Now send in Mr. Happy!" McSquizzy declared.

"Who?" Boog asked.

Deni rose in the air clutching a propane tank. A fierce "Flying Tigers" shark face was painted on its side.

"Go! Go! Go!" Serge shouted.

"I fly! I fly!" Deni answered happily.

Deni hovered over a hunter's truck. He opened his webbed feet and dropped the tank. The animals covered their ears as they waited for the big bang. But there was no big bang. No boom. Not even a fizzle or a pop!

"Aw," McSquizzy groaned. "Mr. Happy didn't go off."

"Hey," Boog said with a shrug, "we were just supposed to run them into town."

"Well, it's time for them to start running, then!" McSquizzy said. He grabbed the still flickering flare from Elliot and loaded it into his undie-slingshot. Then he pulled it back and launched the flare toward the truck and the propane gas tank.

After a few seconds . . .

Boom!

The hunters watched as the truck exploded into a ball of fire. It landed on another truck, starting a chain reaction of exploding vehicles!

The animals oohed and ahhed. Watching the exploding trucks was like watching the most awesome fireworks on the Fourth of July. Even better than that was watching the hunters charging toward town.

"Look at them run!" Boog cheered.

"Sweet!" Giselle said.

"Freedom!" McSquizzy declared.

Boog smiled as he walked to the middle of the battlefield. He had led his troops to victory. The animals had defeated the hunters. The forest was theirs at last!

I love the smell of propane in the morning, Boog thought. Then out of the smoke and fog rang a tiny, jingly tune. Boog knew it at once. It was the song Dinkelman played!

Boog squinted through the thick, soupy smog. Where was it coming from? He took a few steps forward.

"Whoa!" Boog cried. Standing only inches away was Shaw with his shotgun pointed right in Boog's face.

"Hello, Goldilocks!" Shaw sneered.

Chapter Twenty-one

Shaw cocked the trigger. Boog squeezed his eyes shut, waiting for the deadly blast. But instead of hearing a gunshot, Boog heard a loud *whap!*

When Boog opened his eyes, Shaw's hands were empty.

"Huh?" Shaw said.

Boog whirled around and saw Elliot. The deer was sitting on Ian's back, behind a freshly fired underwear slingshot. His buddy had knocked Lorraine right out of Shaw's hands.

"Bull's-eye!" Elliot declared.

Shaw burned with rage. He turned to Boog and attacked him with his bare hands.

"Quick!" Elliot shouted. "We need more ammo!"

The animals loaded their slingshots. More camping gear was hurled fast and furiously. But instead of hitting Shaw, the items hit Boog!

"Elliot!" Boog cried. "Stop helping me!"

The ammo kept coming. Boog saw stars as he was smacked in the head by a fire extinguisher, an iron coffee pot, and even a snowshoe.

Shaw whipped out a sharp knife. "All right, mama's bear, you can do better than that," he sneered. "Let's see what you got!"

"Oh, no!" Boog cried as he ducked.

Elliot hurled a golf club from the slingshot. Boog reached up and snatched it out of the air. He smacked Shaw with the club and sent him flying!

"Oof!" Shaw grunted as he hit the ground.

"Don't mess with the Boogster!" Boog taunted. Then he lifted the golf club and shouted, "Fore!"

Like an evil cat with nine lives, Shaw sprung to his feet. He picked up his gun and pointed it at Boog.

"All right, Lorraine," Shaw told his rifle. "Let's kiss this bear good night!"

Boog dropped the golf club and fell back.

Elliot knew he had to do something, but they were out of ammo. So he jumped into the slingshot and shouted, "Help meeee!"

The animals grabbed Elliot's tail and stretched him all the way back. Then they launched Elliot like a four-legged rocket straight toward Shaw.

"Aaaaahh!" Elliot screamed as he flew through the air. He slammed into the hunter just as Shaw fired the shot.

Bam!

Elliot crash-landed on the ground. He didn't move.

Boog stared at the lifeless body of his friend. His fear turned into rage. And the gentle bear turned into a snarling, ferocious grizzly!

Boog lifted Shaw high into the air. Then with a mighty roar he slammed him hard on the ground.

Shaw trembled as he lay pinned on the ground. He looked up into Boog's gaping mouth. Sharp teeth glistened right above his sorry face.

"No!" Shaw pleaded.

The scene was a blur as Boog took care of Shaw. The animals watched and wondered. Was Boog mauling the hunter? Ripping him to pieces? Turning him inside out?

But when Boog stepped back, Shaw was alive, hog-tied to his beloved rifle, Lorraine.

Boog ran straight to Elliot. He turned him over and whispered, "Buddy?"

Elliot's eyes stayed closed.

"Oh, Elliot!" Boog cried.

He covered his face with his paws and began to sob. Elliot was his buddy! The only other friend he had beside Beth! What would he do now?

A groggy voice suddenly murmured, "Hubbada, hubbada, hubbada . . . "

"Huh?" Boog said. He uncovered his eyes and looked down at Elliot. The bleary deer was coming to!

"Are you all right, Elliot?" Boog asked.

Elliot's one good antler cracked and fell off. "I'm a bit lightheaded," he said.

Boog laughed with joy. He and Elliot were buddies again. Buddies for life!

"Nice show, tiny!" Reilly called out.

The animals cheered for Elliot and Boog.

"Behold!" Boog declared. "The mighty grizzly!"

But the creatures of the wild weren't finished yet. Next they declared open season— on Shaw!

The animals charged toward the hunter, pelting

him with pots, pans, and porcupine quills. For the big finish, they doused him with sticky maple syrup and pillow feathers.

Boog helped Elliot to his feet. "You know, Elliot," he said, "this place really isn't so bad."

"Hold that thought," Elliot said. He struck a karate pose. Then he ran to karate chop Shaw.

Suddenly Boog heard a *putt-putt-putt* sound.

Glancing up, he spotted a Ranger Service helicopter flying overhead. The animals stopped beating Shaw to watch the chopper land. They dropped Shaw and scurried in different directions into the woods. Shaw hobbled into the woods himself, like a wounded and hunted animal.

Boog didn't run. He walked toward the helicopter and watched as the door swung open. A bright, smiling face peered out. It was the face Boog thought he'd never see again . . .

"Beth?"

Chapter Twenty-two

"Boog?" Beth asked.

Carefully, she took a few steps forward. Boog's fur was dirty and matted. He didn't look like the big cuddly bear she dropped off in the wild three days ago. Had he changed for the worse? Had he become ferocious? Did he remember her?

Beth and Boog came face-to-face. They stared deeply into each other's eyes. Then Boog's tongue darted out and licked Beth's face from top to bottom!

"Oh, Boog!" Beth laughed.

She wrapped her arms around the bear and gave him a big hug. The other animals couldn't believe their eyes. Why was Boog—their mighty and ferocious leader—hugging a human?

"What's he doing?" Reilly asked.

"Isn't he going to maul her?" McSquizzy asked.

"No!" Elliot explained. "That's Boog's mom. And she's going to take him home."

Beth smiled up at Boog and said, "Come on. I'm bringing you back home with me."

Home?

Boog watched Beth walk back to the helicopter. For the last three days all he wanted was to go back home. Why couldn't he bring himself to follow?

He looked back at Elliot, then at Dinkelman on the ground. Using his teeth, Boog picked up the teddy bear. Then he walked after Beth.

Elliot's heart broke into a million pieces. How could Boog go without him? "Oh, no!" He groaned.

Boog stopped in front of Beth with Dinkelman between his teeth.

"Come on, Boog," Beth said. "Let's go home."

Boog opened his jaws. Dinkelman dropped into Beth's hands.

"Boog?" Beth asked, staring at the teddy bear. "What are you trying to tell me?"

Boog looked back at the animals, peeking out from trees and bushes. Beth smiled as she began to understand. Boog didn't need to go home.

Boog *was* home!

She wrapped her arms around Boog and hugged him hard.

"I'm so proud of you, Boog, but I am going to miss you!" Beth said.

Elliot brightened when he saw Boog walk back. He was coming for him!

"How are we both going to fit in the helicopter?" Elliot asked excitedly. His eyes popped wide open as the chopper lifted off the ground. "She's coming back for us, isn't she?"

"Who?" Boog asked.

Elliot stared at Boog. "The shorts lady!" he said. "What's going on?"

Boog didn't answer.

He smiled as he joined the other animals. They were still having fun with the hunting gear. Reilly and the beavers were hauling over another propane tank. Ian was sporting a brand-new flannel hunter's vest. Maria was carrying Serge on her black-and-white striped back.

"I know he's a duck!" Maria told Rosie. "But he treats me like a lady!"

Elliot still didn't get it. The lady with the shorts was their only ticket out of the forest.

"Come on, Boog!" Elliot said. "What's our pickup time?"

"Elliot, we're staying here," Boog said. "This is our home, these are our people, this is where we reside."

Elliot's jaw dropped open. Did all those knocks on the head make Boog crazy?

"Where have you been for the last few days, Boog?" Elliot cried. "This place is horrible. Horrible!"

"Oh, come on, Elliot," Boog said. "It's not that bad."

Elliot tried to get a grip. "She's at least going to bring us some Woo-Hoo bars," he asked. "Right?"

"It's just the two of us, Elliot," Boog said. "Unless you plan on going back to your herd."

Elliot couldn't imagine leaving Boog. They were buddies. A team. Boogster and the Incredible Mister E.

"No way!" Elliot said. "Bros before does!"

"Hello, Elliot," a voice cut in.

"Huh?" Elliot said. He turned to look at Giselle. His crush smiled at him as she strolled by.

Elliot smiled back.

"Er—catch you later, Boog!" Elliot said. He ran after Giselle.

Crash!

A tree fell down, right in front of Boog.

Glancing back, Boog saw Reilly. With a buck-toothy grin the beaver held up a chain saw and shouted, "Timber!"

"Hey!" McSquizzy shouted as he trotted by on Mr. Weenie's back. "Get off my trees!"

"Yes, indeed, feels like home, baby!" Boog said.

He leaned against the fallen tree and grinned. He didn't need a garage anymore. Or his kibble dish. Or a cushy little bed. Or even a hit stage show with adoring fans. All Boog really needed was the lush greenery of a majestic forest, sparkling waters, friends for life . . .

"Oof!" Boog grunted as something soft and squishy hit him in the face.

. . . and a good rabbit fight!